Hot Dogs and Homicide
A Nanny Blu Cozy Mystery

Summer in Diamond Bay
Book 4

By

Maci Grant

TABLE OF CONTENTS

CHAPTER 1...7

CHAPTER 2... 13

CHAPTER 3... 19

CHAPTER 4... 25

CHAPTER 5... 31

CHAPTER 6... 37

CHAPTER 7... 41

CHAPTER 8... 45

CHAPTER 9... 49

CHAPTER 10 55

CHAPTER 11 61

CHAPTER 12 67

CHAPTER 13 73

CHAPTER 14 77

CHAPTER 15 85

CHAPTER 16 91

CHAPTER 17 97

CHAPTER 18 103

CHAPTER 19 109

CHAPTER 20 113

CHAPTER 21 119

CHAPTER 22 125

CHAPTER 23 131

CHAPTER 24 137

CHAPTER 25 143

CHAPTER 26 147

CHAPTER 27 153

CHAPTER 28 159

CHAPTER 29 165

CHAPTER 30 169

CHAPTER 1

Dark yellow mustard streamed across the hot dog. Blu smiled at the scent. Her stomach rumbled in anticipation of eating it. Marley and Joey clamored beside her, just as eager to have their own hot dogs.

"Thanks so much." Blu paid the man behind the cart. "Where's the usual guy?"

"Oh, my dad?" The young man shrugged. "He's letting me man the cart today."

"Well, good job." Blu smiled. "I have to say that this is one of the things we look forward to the most when we come to visit the lighthouse. All three of us love the hot dogs."

"I'm glad. I'll be sure to pass on the compliment." He handed a hot dog to Joey, then another to Blu for Marley. "Enjoy, kids."

"Thank you." Joey smiled.

"Yum!" Marley opened her mouth to take a bite.

"Wait! Marley, it might be too hot. Why don't we sit

on that bench over there and eat them?"

Blu led the kids to a small green bench that faced the ocean. She handed out juice boxes and opened her own bottle of water. While they ate, the kids swung their feet. Blu stared out across the ocean. When she finished her hot dog she tossed the wrapper into the nearby trashcan.

The tall lighthouse grabbed her attention. She looked up at the large glass panels that sparkled in the sunlight. It was a small lighthouse, but it was a favorite destination for Blu and the kids. "Finish up so we can get inside before it closes."

Blu checked her watch. She knew the lighthouse closed at four and it was already three-thirty. She collected the hot dog wrappers from the kids and tossed them in the garbage. Then she scrubbed their faces and hands with wipes.

"Marley, I think you got more ketchup on you than the hot dog did."

"Oops." Marley giggled.

"Can we get another, Blu? Can we, please?" Joey stood up.

"Not now, Joey or we won't have time to see the lighthouse. Maybe when we come back out."

"Okay." Joey sighed.

Blu took Marley's hand and walked the kids into the lighthouse. They paid for their tickets.

Before heading for the spiral stairs, Blu walked with the kids around the exhibits. Although school was out for the summer, she always liked to incorporate a little education into their activities.

"Look at this. This is what the lighthouse looked like fifty years ago." She tapped a picture that was protected by a glass display case.

Before the kids could look, a woman rushed down the stairs. She was tall, thin, and moved so fast that Blu almost thought she was a ghost. She ran right out the door of the lighthouse. Blu narrowed her eyes. Screams alerted her that something bad had happened outside.

"What's going on?" Joey looked toward the door with wide eyes. "Why are people screaming?"

Marley covered her ears.

"Don't worry about that." Blu pointed to the picture. "Take a look at this."

The screams subsided. The kids looked at the picture. Blu peeked out through the front window of the museum just in time to see a body being covered by a white sheet. Her heart raced. It looked as if someone had jumped off the top of the lighthouse.

She met the eyes of the man behind the counter, who had grown pale. "Is there a back door?"

"Yes, right this way." He led her to the back door. As curious as Blu was about what had happened, she didn't want the kids to see the body.

"Blu, why are we leaving? We didn't even get to climb the stairs!" Joey frowned.

"Next time, Joey. I was wrong. The museum is

already closing."

"Yes, we changed the hours." The clerk cleared his throat. "Listen to your mother."

"She's my nanny."

"Then listen to your nanny."

Blu steered the kids away from the lighthouse. As she walked with them, she noticed that the hot dog cart was gone. She thought about the woman whom she'd seen. Was she with the man who'd jumped? Her stomach twisted at the thought.

Just as she was about to cross the street toward the parking lot where her car was parked, a patrol car glided to a stop beside her.

"Blu?" Chief Pitman stuck his head out the window. "Were you at the lighthouse?"

"Yes, I was."

"She wouldn't let us climb the stairs!" Joey pouted. "And I wanted another hot dog."

"Joey, shush." Blu frowned.

"Anything I should know?" Chief Pitman met her eyes.

"I saw a woman. She was tall and thin. She ran down the stairs and out the door."

"About what age, do you think?"

"I don't know. Young. Maybe twenty?"

"Thanks, Blu."

"Wait. Chief Pitman, do you know who it was? I mean, the reason why you're here?" She glanced at the kids to indicate caution.

"Ah, yes. It was Emile Grover."

"Emile?" Blu's eyes widened. "The owner of the hot dog cart?"

"Yes."

"Oh, his poor son." Blu put her hand to her mouth. "He must have seen the whole thing."

"It's a terrible thing. We're going to get it all sorted out."

Blu shook her head. "Is there ever an explanation for something like that?"

"Not a good one, I'm afraid."

The patrol car pulled off.

Blu was feeling anxious as she helped the kids into the car. Once they were settled she called Maddie on her cell phone.

"Hi, Blu. How is the lighthouse?"

"Horrible. The hot dog cart owner jumped off the lighthouse." She lowered her voice to be sure the kids couldn't hear her.

"What? How horrible! Did the kids see?"

"No, but they're both mad at me for making them leave early."

"I bet. You can bring them over here to distract them if you want."

"Great! Thanks, Maddie. We'll be there in fifteen."

"We'll be waiting for you. Chrissa, stop hitting your brother with a pillow!"

Blu smiled as she hung up the phone. Maddie had her hands full with the two kids she nannied for, a ten-year-old girl and a twelve-year-old boy. Blu considered herself lucky to only have a moody seven-year-old and a precocious four-year-old to juggle.

When she got into the car Joey scowled at her from the backseat.

"I know that you're both disappointed about the lighthouse. But we're going to go to the Rosses' house. Alright?"

"Alright!" Joey smiled from ear to ear. "I can't wait to see Brennan."

"Chrissa will do my toes!" Marley wiggled her toes.

Blu smiled and drove out of the parking lot. She looked back toward the flashing lights and gathered crowd. She couldn't think of a single reason why Emile would take his life. But, then again, she barely knew the man.

CHAPTER 2

When Blu arrived at the beach house that Maddie's family stayed in for the summer, her mind instantly returned to Emile. It bothered her in a way that she couldn't shake.

"Hi!" Maddie waved them into the house. Brennan was curled up on the couch with a tablet. Chrissa already had her make-up and nail polish kit out.

"Oh, my customer is here!" Chrissa wiggled her fingers at Marley.

Marley ran straight for her. Joey plopped down on the couch next to Brennan and did his best to look just as cool.

"You doing okay?" Maddie met Blu's eyes.

"I'm okay. I just can't believe it. All I keep thinking about is how his son was there. What kind of thing is that for a son to witness?"

"Horrible." Maddie shook her head. "If he wanted to end it all, why did he do it in front of his kid? That's just cruel.''

Blu's cell phone rang. When she checked, she saw that it was Chief Pitman calling.

"Hello?"

"Blu, I need you to come down to the station."

"Why?"

"This wasn't a suicide. Emile was thrown off of the top of the lighthouse. I want to discuss this woman that you saw and anything else you might have seen. Can you come in?"

Blu glanced at the kids, who were both happily engaged. "Maddie, do you mind watching the kids?"

"No, it's fine."

"I can be there in a few minutes, Chief Pitman."

"As fast as you can. This entire case just got turned on its head."

As Blu drove to the police station her heart pounded. Was it possible that the woman she saw run past had something to do with Emile's death?

She parked at the police station and hurried in. Chief Pitman greeted her at the door.

"Come with me. I don't want any interruptions." He led her into one of the interrogation rooms and closed the door.

When Blu heard the click of the door as it closed, she began to feel a little uncomfortable. Although Chief Pitman appeared to want her help, he still intimidated her a bit.

"Sit." He gestured to the chair.

Blu sat down and looked across the table at him. "How do you know it was murder?"

"When the medical examiner arrived at the scene he pointed out that Emile could not have jumped and landed in the position that he'd fallen in. Also Emile's collar was torn." He sat down across from her and sighed. "So what was a simple suicide has now become a murder. You're my best witness so far. So let's hear it."

"I already told you what I saw."

"You said that Emile's son was operating the hot dog cart when you arrived at the lighthouse?"

"Yes he was. I asked him where his father was. He said that his father had let him take over the cart that day. If he knew his father was in the lighthouse, he didn't mention it to me."

"The funny thing is that when I arrived, the cart was gone and so was Emile's son, Oliver. We've yet to be able to find him, although to be fair we haven't been looking for too long," said Chief Pitman.

"I saw him leaving right after the body—uh, after Emile fell. I figured he was spooked by it. But..."

"But?" Chief Pitman leaned forward.

"From where he was, I don't see how he wouldn't have seen his father fall. If he knew it was his father, then why would he pack up and leave?"

"That's a very good question, and as soon as we find Oliver we're going to ask him that. Right now I'd like you to tell me about the woman that you saw."

Blu shook her head. "I already told you what I saw. But I really don't think that she could have done it."

"Oh? She was at the top of the lighthouse at the time that he fell."

"Maybe, but she was very thin—not just skinny, but rail thin. I've been up to the top of that lighthouse plenty of times, and there is a thick metal railing that surrounds it. I can't see her getting Emile over that railing. He was a very large man."

"You may be right. But seeing is not always the truth. Perhaps she was stronger than she seemed. Either way I need to talk to her. She didn't say anything to you?"

"No. Not at all." Blu frowned. "Isn't there some kind of surveillance system on the top of the lighthouse? I remember last summer one of the staff members showed it to the kids. It records weather data also."

"Yes, it's still there, but unfortunately, before the murder occurred someone disabled it. There was visible damage to it. That is another reason we're considering this a murder. Someone knew the camera was there and broke it on purpose."

"Without an image, I don't see how you're going to find her."

"I'm going to have you sit with my sketch artist."

"Okay. I can do that. But I only saw her for a moment."

"Just do the best you can. In the meantime I'm going

to keep trying to track down Oliver."

CHAPTER 3

When Chief Pitman left the room, a woman stepped inside. She offered Blu an awkward smile.

"Hi, hello—uh, I'm the sketch artist."

"Okay." Blu mustered a small smile. It went against her instincts to smile when she was upset.

The woman sat down across from her and opened a large sketchbook. She spread out a few pencils beside it. The pencils began to roll right off the table.

"Oh no, stop!" The woman grabbed the pencils just before they reached the edge.

Something about the entire scenario caused a laugh to bubble up from within Blu.

"Sorry about that. I'm Allison, by the way."

"Blu."

"It's nice to meet you Blu. I'm rather new at this. But don't think that means I can't do it, because I can. I just can't always keep track of my pencils." She smiled. "Now, can you tell me what this woman looked like?"

"She was tall and thin. That's about all I remember."

"What about her hair?"

"It was long, I guess. Past her shoulders."

"Don't tell me lines and shapes, tell me textures."

"Textures?" Blu raised an eyebrow.

"Yes—like her skin. Was it smooth? Bumpy? Weathered? Her hair. Was it stiff, smooth, frizzy?" She ran the pencil along the sketchbook.

"I only saw her for a moment."

"Just close your eyes. The human mind retains much more information than our conscious mind recognizes. In that moment that you saw the woman you took a photograph of her. You just have to be able to access it. Take a deep breath and just relax."

Blu sighed. She wasn't sure if she could relax with four concrete walls around her. She closed her eyes and took a deep breath. "Okay."

"What do you remember the most?"

"She was so tall, so thin—she looked like a ghost coming down the stairs."

"What made her look that way?"

"I guess the way her hair drifted. It was long and light—and thin."

"Okay, that's good. What about her age? Did you get an idea of how old she might be?"

"Young. I don't know exactly, but young."

"Younger than you?"

Blu blinked. Despite being under thirty she had not considered herself young in a long time. "Yes, younger than me. Much. Maybe about twenty or even younger."

"Okay, this is great, thank you. Her complexion? Was it pale, tan, olive?"

"Tan. A deep tan."

"Perfect, thank you. Here we go." She turned the sketch around to show Blu. "Does that look like her?"

Blu stared at the sketch. Even though it was done with only shading and a small amount of color the image was nearly identical to the woman. "Yes. That's her. You're amazing."

"Oh, well, thank you." She looked away shyly. "I try. I'll get this to Chief Pitman so that he can put it out there. Hopefully we'll be able to identify her quickly."

"I hope so." Blu frowned. "I feel so terrible about Emile. I guess it's a little strange that I feel so much grief over a man I hardly knew. But it isn't just about Emile, I guess. It's about what he stood for—lighthearted fun, good food, an innocent time at the beach. All of that goes with him."

"I don't think that's strange at all. Even if you don't get to know a person on a deep level they can still have a huge impact on you. I never met Emile, but the way you talk about him lets me know that he was a man with a passion for his work—for making people happy, for offering that innocent beach experience. That tells me a lot about him. Any loss of life is tragic, but when it hits so close, that makes it even harder to understand."

"You're very insightful. Thank you. I feel a little better."

"Well, you're going to feel great when this picture finds our mystery lady."

As Allison left the room Blu smiled. It wasn't forced. She stood and followed after her. In the hall outside of the interrogation room she bumped right into Chief Pitman.

"Oh, I'm sorry, I didn't see you there."

"It's quite alright. I was just coming to get you. I managed to find Oliver and I'm about to question him. I'd like for you to observe through the mirror."

"Me?" Blu's eyes widened.

"Yes, Blu. I think you've shown me that your instincts are very good. Plus you're the only person in this police station that has spoken to Oliver. You have a slight advantage over me. You know how Oliver was acting in the moments before his father died. I'm going to show him this sketch, and see if he recognizes the person."

"I'm glad to help."

"Good. Just in here." He opened the door to a narrow room.

One wall was mostly taken up by a large two-way mirror. Blu could see Oliver through the mirror. He sat behind a small metal table. If possible, he looked even younger than he had when she saw him earlier that day. His skin was pale, his eyes downcast. Blu noticed that he had folded his hands so tight on the table in front of him that his knuckles were turning white.

Her heart ached for him. She couldn't imagine how

she would handle her own father's death. It would not be good.

CHAPTER 4

Chief Pitman opened the door and walked into the room with Oliver.

"Well, son, it's been quite a day." He sat down across from Oliver.

Oliver glanced up at him and then quickly away.

"Why am I here?"

"Is that how you're going to play this, Oliver?" Chief Pitman leaned across the table toward him. "As if you don't know what happened today."

"I don't. Some cop just snagged me off the street and brought me here. No one will tell me why I'm here. What did I do?" He looked up at Chief Pitman again. "Am I going to jail?"

Blu stepped closer to the glass. Was it really possible that Oliver didn't know it was his father that had fallen from the lighthouse?

"Were you at the lighthouse today?"

"Yes, sir."

"Are you aware of the death that occurred there?"

"Uh, yes. I mean, I thought he was probably dead. I

took off when it happened. Is that it? Am I in trouble for leaving?"

"Oliver." Chief Pitman waited until Oliver met his eyes. "The man who died today was your father, Emile."

"What?" Oliver stood up so fast that he knocked his chair over in the process.

Chief Pitman stood up as well with one hand placed on his weapon.

"That's impossible! It was not my father! Why are you lying to me?"

"Oliver, I need you to calm down. There are about three police officers right outside this door and if they think for one second that you may pose a danger to me, they will come in and cuff you. Understand?"

"No. I don't understand any of this. Why are you saying that man was my father?"

"It was, Oliver. He's been positively identified. I'm not lying to you, son. I know this is a shock, but I am telling you the truth."

"And I'm telling you that it couldn't have been him. I was running the hot dog cart because he was supposed to be meeting with an investor."

"Was he having a hard time financially?"

"Just like everyone else. But why would he tell me that he was going to be somewhere else? My father doesn't lie."

"Everyone lies, son. Some of us try not to, but we all do it. So you're telling me that you had no idea that your father was in the lighthouse?"

"No." Oliver stared into the empty space between them. "No, I didn't. Are you sure it's him?"

"I'm afraid so."

Oliver's chin began to tremble. His eyes squinted at the corners. His hands balled into fists on the table. "Why? Why did this happen?"

"I'm going to try to figure that out, Oliver. But I need your help."

Chief Pitman seemed to giving the young man several minutes to calm down as Oliver sobbed into his hands at the table. When he finally looked back up at him, the chief continued with his questions. "Did you notice anything unusual today? Maybe a strange customer? Or someone you recognized?"

"No." He shook his head and tightened his eyes. "No, it was just a normal day."

"How about this woman?" He placed the sketch on the table in front of Oliver. "Do you know her?"

Oliver's face drained of color. He looked away from the photograph. "I don't know her. I've never seen her."

"Really?" Chief Pitman stood up and walked around the side of the table. "Take another look. Hm?" He leaned over Oliver's shoulder.

Oliver looked back at the sketch for a long moment. Blu watched as his lips tensed and his throat buckled with a hard swallow.

"I don't know her. Please. I need to tell my mother

what's happened."

"She already knows, Oliver. Unlike you, she was rather easy to find. So why did you run and hide, Oliver? Was it because you were involved?"

"Involved with my father's suicide?" Oliver's eyes widened. "How? By disappointing him? By not being the son he hoped for?"

"Oliver, your father didn't commit suicide." Chief Pitman stepped back to allow the young man some space.

"But you said he fell from the lighthouse."

"More accurately he was pushed—or thrown. Something that a person would do in a rage."

"He was killed?" Oliver's voice grew dark. "Who would do that? He's never hurt anyone."

"I don't know, Oliver. That's what I'm trying to find out. But first, what I would like to understand is: why would a son flee his father's side?"

"I didn't know it was him. I didn't know." Oliver covered his eyes with one hand and released a growl. "I just didn't want to be there. I thought my father would want me to leave so that no one would associate the cart with tragedy. I thought I was doing the right thing."

"If you are such a good and honorable son, then why did you hide out? It shouldn't have been that hard for us to find you."

"I wasn't hiding out. I just had some things to take care of."

"What things?"

Oliver lowered his hand. Blu could see the moisture of tears in his eyes. "Things."

"Listen, son, you were at the scene of the crime."

"Are you accusing me?" Oliver stood up again. "People saw me there. They saw me standing there, so how could I have done anything?"

"I don't know, Oliver. But that's what I'm going to find out. Now are you sure that you don't know who this woman is?" He pushed the sketch back toward him.

"I told you I don't know." Oliver swept the sketch off the table and onto the floor. "Stop asking me!"

"Calm down. I'll get you some water." Chief Pitman opened the door of the room. "I'll be back." He closed the door.

CHAPTER 5

Blu watched Oliver pick up the sketch off the floor. He stared at it for a moment, then placed it back on the table. The way he handled it—the soft touch of his fingertips, the careful way he put it down on the table—told her something.

"He knows who she is."

"You think so?" Chief Pitman stepped into the room with her. "Then why isn't he talking?"

"I don't know." Blu shook her head. "I don't think he's faking that grief, though."

"It's hard to say, isn't it?"

"It always is. But he seemed genuinely surprised when you told him that it was his father who'd died."

"Yes, I'd agree with that."

"I do think he knows, though, exactly who it is in that picture. You should question him about it again."

"I have a better idea. I'm going to let him go."

"What?" Blu turned to face him. "Why would you do that?"

"Because when I let him go he's going to lead us right

to this mystery woman. I'll put one of my guys on him to watch his every move."

"Is that legal?"

"Did I ever tell you that you ask far too many questions?" Chief Pitman winked at her, then stepped out of the room.

Blu stared after him. She wondered if the amount of trust she'd begun to have in Chief Pitman was well placed.

She looked back through the mirror at Oliver. He rested his head on his folded arms. His shoulders were limp and his face hidden. It was clear that he was defeated by what had happened in the room. Yet he hadn't given Chief Pitman a name for the woman in the sketch. Which communicated to Blu that whoever the woman in the picture was, she was incredibly important to Oliver. Important enough to turn a blind eye to her involvement in his father's murder?

Blu headed back to Maddie's to collect the kids. It was getting late and she didn't want Maddie to get into trouble for having two extra kids at the house.

When she arrived, Maddie opened the door for her.

"Now don't get mad."

"What?" Blu's heart flipped.

"I swear, I only looked away from them for a moment, but I guess it was long enough."

Blu's eyes widened when she saw that four-year-old

Marley's hair had bright pink streaks in it.

"Oh no, no, no!" Blu gasped and grabbed a handful of Marley's hair. "Is it marker or something? Will it wash out?"

"I don't want to wash it out!" Marley huffed.

"Sure it'll wash out—in a few days. It's just a little temporary hair dye. What's the big deal?" Chrissa shrugged. "I use it in my hair all of the time."

"You're ten, Chrissa, and you have your mother's permission. That's the big deal," Maddie said and then turned back toward Blu. "I'm so sorry." She cringed. "You can tell Rachel it was my fault. I'll even call her if you want."

"No. It's okay." Blu cleared her throat. "Where's Joey?"

Joey walked out of Brennan's room and into the living room. His hair was still the same color. "Hi, Blu."

"Hi, Joey. Get your things we have to go." Blu looked at Marley's hair again and tried not to scream. There was no doubt in her mind that Rachel was going to be quite upset.

"Blu, I'm really, really sorry." Maddie met her eyes.

"Maddie, it's no big deal. These things happen with kids. It's okay."

"You're not mad?"

"It is what it is." Blu shrugged. "There's nothing that can be done now."

"But you trusted me and—"

"—And they're kids, Maddie. It's not your fault." Blu hugged her. "Don't stress."

"Thanks." Maddie sighed with relief.

Blu smiled, but the moment she got on the other side of the door she pulled out a baby wipe and started to scrub at Marley's hair.

"That's not working." Joey peered at Blu's scrubbing hand.

"I can see that, Joey."

"It's still not working."

"Thanks, Joey."

"Blu?"

"What?" She looked up at him.

"I don't think it's going to work."

Blu sighed. Marley's hair was just as pink. She ushered them into the car and drove home as slowly as possible. In her mind, she recited all of the excuses that she could come up with, but in the end she knew that she would tell Rachel the truth—at least most of the truth. She always tried to be as honest as possible with her employers.

She parked in the driveway and marched the kids into the house. She was prepared to face the consequences. When she walked into the living room she found Rachel sound asleep on the sofa.

"Let's go get baths, kids." She hurried them up the stairs to the bathroom.

As she ran the water for Marley's bath, the sound of the rushing water coming out of the faucet relaxed her.

Her mind filled with memories of Oliver's face. No matter what Chief Pitman thought, she was sure that Oliver knew nothing about his father's death. With no other lead to follow up on, she hoped that Chief Pitman would be able to get to the bottom of things, but she had a suspicion that she was going to have to do some serious investigating of her own.

After she tucked the children into bed, Blu walked back into the living room. She covered Rachel with a blanket and collected the empty glass of wine from the coffee table.

Rachel spent quite a bit of time alone these days, as her husband was often on business trips or in the city. Rachel handled it well, but from Blu's point of view, it was clear that she missed her husband.

Blu took some time to wash the dishes and straighten up the kitchen, then she headed to bed herself. When she switched out the light she caught a glimpse of the lighthouse in the distance. Its steady light still glowed out across the water. Her heart sank.

It wasn't the peaceful alluring sight that it had once been. Now it had a darker memory. She hoped that solving Emile's murder would change that.

CHAPTER 6

Early the next morning Blu's cell phone rang. She rolled over in bed and stared at the glow of it. For a moment she considered throwing it against the wall. Instead, she dutifully picked it up. Right away she saw that it was Chief Pitman.

"Morning, Chief."

"Morning, Blu. I'm sorry if I woke you."

"It's okay. What is it?"

"I was going over the interview from yesterday. I'm pretty sure that Oliver knows who that woman in the picture is."

"No bites yet, hm?"

"No one seems to have any idea who she is."

"No one but Oliver."

"That's what I'm thinking. But I might have played my hand a little rough and spooked him."

"You think he's afraid to talk to you?"

"I think he wouldn't talk to me if I was the last man on earth. So I've asked AJ to help me out. He's going to host a buck-a-beer fundraiser to generate support for the family. I'm betting that young Oliver will be there. I'd like you to be there as well—as a fly on the wall, so to speak."

"Chief Pitman?'

"Yes?"

"Is your plan to get him drunk and then have me see if I can get him to talk?"

"Fly on the wall, Blu. That's all I'm asking for."

"I think I can handle that. What time?"

"I'll text you the time as soon as I confirm things with AJ."

"Thanks."

Blu hung up the phone and pulled herself out of bed. She knew that Rachel would notice Marley's hair and there would be some explaining to do. After dressing she walked down the hall to wake the kids. When she poked her head into Marley's room, the little girl was not in her bed.

"Marley?" Blu's heart lurched.

"We're in the kitchen, Blu."

Rachel's voice made Blu's heart pound again. Would she be angry?

When she stepped into the kitchen she saw that Joey was at the table as well. Both kids had bowls of their favorite cereal in front of them.

"Rachel, about Marley's hair, I'm so sorry."

"Don't worry about it." Rachel poured her a cup of coffee.

"Really?"

"Sure." She shrugged. "Pink happens. Right, Marley?"

"Right." Marley nodded.

Blu was relieved. She accepted the mug of coffee. "Thank you."

"Why don't you take the day off? I'm going to take her to my stylist and see if there is anything she can do."

"I'm very sorry, Rachel."

"Blu, it's okay. When Joey was three I didn't want to cut his hair. I thought it was so cute to put his hair in a ponytail and show him off. Well, one day I took him to a play date with a friend of mine. Her five-year-old decided he needed a haircut and my little Joey came back to me with his ponytail in his hand. Even if the stylist can't get the pink out, it will be fine. Just enjoy your day, Blu. Alright?"

"Thanks." Blu frowned. Even though Rachel was being kind and didn't seem too upset, Blu suspected that she was just hiding it well. Or perhaps something else was weighing on her mind. Either way the knit of Rachel's brow and the tension in her voice made Blu think that something was off.

She was relieved to have the day off to investigate, but wished it were for a different reason. As she grabbed her keys her cell phone rang.

"Chief Pitman?"

"No, it's me, Maddie. How did the hair situation go?"

"I think it will be fine."

"Oh, good. That's a relief. What are you doing?"

"I have the day off."

"Really? Chrissa's nails get chipped and I'm docked a day's pay. You come home with a pink-haired child and score the day off?"

"Rachel is quite kind. Though I do think she might be more upset than she's letting on."

"Let's hope not. The kids have tennis this morning. Do you want to catch a quick breakfast?"

"Sure, that would be great."

"There's a coffee shop near the sports complex."

"I know it. I'll be there in ten minutes."

"Great, see you soon."

Blu tucked her phone into her pocket. She opened the door to the car and dropped down into the driver's seat. As she backed out of the driveway the flicker of light and scenery in her peripheral vision made her think of the moment that she saw the woman flee from the stairs. Blu shook her head in an attempt to clear it.

The street she drove down was lined with large beach houses. Each one seemed to compete with the next when it came to extravagance and luxury. But that wasn't the real beach, not the one that existed all year round.

That beach belonged to Emile and his hot dog cart, and all of the other vendors that lived for the tourists but still continued to survive throughout the rest of the year. If Emile was struggling financially he didn't have too many options.

CHAPTER 7

When Blu arrived at the cafe, she tried to brighten her mood. She wanted to enjoy her time with Maddie.

Maddie waved to her through the large front window of the small restaurant.

Blu smiled and pulled open the door. She walked right over to the booth and plopped down beside her best friend

"So glad you could meet me. I feel like we never get a chance to hang out without the kids."

"Then you should meet me at the Beach Bum tonight. AJ is hosting a dollar-a-beer fundraiser for the Grovers."

"Oh, AJ, huh? I bet you're looking forward to seeing him."

"Maybe." Blu grinned. "Although I wish it was under different circumstances. I keep thinking about Emile's wife and son." Blu detailed everything she knew about the crime and Oliver's interrogation. She hoped that Maddie could give her a new perspective on the case.

After they ordered breakfast, Maddie seemed to be mulling over the information.

"The obvious suspect would be the son. You're sure that Oliver wasn't involved?'

"I think that Chief Pitman still has his suspicions, but I don't see how he could have gotten from the hot dog cart to the top of the lighthouse in such a short time. I never saw him go past me up the stairs. I don't see how he could have done it."

"Hm. It seems very strange that he wouldn't know that his father was there, though. Why would Emile tell his son that he was going to a business meeting and then end up at the very place where Oliver was?" Maddie sipped her coffee and stared off into space for a moment. "It's a very odd scenario."

"Yes, it is. I keep running through it in my mind—what it would have been like if I hadn't looked around the museum with the kids for a few minutes before it happened. Part of me is grateful we weren't up there to see it happen, but part of me wonders if I could have saved Emile."

"Aw, Blu, you can't think that way. I'm glad the kids weren't there to witness it. That's something they would never forget."

"Yes, you're right." Blu narrowed her eyes. "I am determined to find out what happened, though."

"I think it's intriguing that the woman you saw had an impact on Oliver. Who do you think she is?"

"I don't know. A friend? A girlfriend? Maybe a relative?" Blu smiled at the waitress as she set down a plate of food in front of her. "Thank you."

"You're sure he recognized her?"

"I'm sure. But he also seemed surprised. If he knew her, and she was involved, I would think that he would be aware of it. Instead, he looked surprised when he saw the sketch."

"So the plan tonight is to try to get him to talk about her?"

"Yes." Blu frowned. "I get the feeling Chief Pitman expects me to flirt with him or something."

"Is that so bad?"

"He's just a kid, Maddie."

"Blu, you're not an old lady, you know. He's only a few years younger than you."

"Maybe so, but to me he's a kid."

"I'll be there with you to aid in the flirtation." Maddie winked.

"I hope that we'll be able to find something out."

"What about the wife?"

"Hm?"

"Well, in cases like this, isn't it always the wife?" Maddie pushed her eggs across her plate.

"I hadn't really thought about it. I know that Chief Pitman notified her already. He didn't seem to suspect her. Now that you mention it, though, I think I might go see her for myself. I know she runs a shop in town."

"Just be careful."

"Always." Blu winked.

As they finished their meals, the two chatted about the fundraiser that night. Blu was more than a little bit distracted by the thought of getting to see AJ. As much as she was trying to prepare herself for the fact that summer would soon be over and AJ would remain at the beach while she returned with the family to the city, she couldn't ignore the subtle ache in her chest. She would miss him—more than she thought she should.

When Blu left the cafe her mind was made up. She wanted to know more about the Grover family. What better way to gain some intimate knowledge than through the matriarch?

Blu opened a search page on her phone and typed in the name Hilda Grover. The address came up in the first few results. She set it as a new destination and waited for the map to appear. Once it had, she began to follow the directions to the address.

The Grover home was only about fifteen minutes away from the beach. Blu parked in front of it. It was a modest but well-kept home. The grass was cut, the garden was tended, and the exterior had recently been painted. The one-story ranch looked just like the one beside it and the one across from it.

Blu walked toward the front door. She noticed that there was only one car in the driveway. If Oliver was home there was no sign of him yet.

CHAPTER 8

Blu knocked on the door. Right away it swung open. Blu suspected that the woman who opened the door had been watching her approach the house. The skin beneath her eyes was puffy and red.

"Hi. Mrs. Grover?"

"Please, call me Hilda." She dabbed at her eyes with a tissue. "Can I help you?"

"I just wanted to offer you my condolences. I didn't know Emile well, but he will be missed."

"Oh, thank you."

Hilda seemed to be eyeing Blu carefully, and Blu guessed that she might, in fact, welcome some company."

As if she were reading Blu's mind, Hilda continued. "Would you like to come in?" She trembled as she blinked back tears. "It's still setting in. I just keep thinking he will walk through that door any minute."

"I'm very sorry, Hilda." Blu reached out and gently took her hand. "If there's anything I can do, please don't be afraid to ask."

"No, there's nothing, really. I mean, he's gone. What can anyone do?" She sighed and passed her gaze over the photographs on the mantle. "It's strange how someone can be there one day and gone the next."

"Yes, it is." Blu followed her gaze to the pictures. She noticed quite a few of Emile and several that featured Oliver. "Your son must be devastated."

"Oh, he is." Hilda nodded and swallowed back a sob. "There's nothing that he wanted more than to please his father. To think that he will never have that chance is heartbreaking."

"It is terrible that he was there when his father passed."

"I still don't understand how it all happened." She sighed and clutched her tissue. "None of it makes any sense to me."

"Did Chief Pitman show you a sketch? Of a woman?"

"Yes, he did. I'm afraid I don't know the woman, though. Emile did have his ways, though…"

"What do you mean?" Blu turned back to face her.

"I mean, Emile liked the ladies. He never paraded them in front of me, but I had my suspicions."

Blu narrowed her eyes. "So you think he was having an affair with the woman in the sketch?"

"Well, no wife likes to think it, but let's be realistic, most men do cheat." She sniffled. "I guess he paid the ultimate price for it."

"I'm sorry, Hilda, that must have been hard to deal with."

"It was alright. We'd been together for so long that we were more like fixtures in one another's lives than romantic partners. You'll understand one day."

Blu frowned. She was determined that would not be the case. But she kept that to herself. "Still, the woman seems rather thin."

"What are you saying?" Hilda crossed her arms.

"Emile was not a small man."

"No he wasn't." Hilda shrugged. "But people can be stronger than they look."

"That's true." Blu looked back at the photographs. "Are you sure you've never seen her before? Not even perhaps with your son? A friend of his from school?"

"Oliver? No." Hilda shook her head. "I've never seen her with him. Oliver is a bit of a loner."

"Really? He seems like such a personable young man."

"Emile was always very strict about who he could associate with. You see, Emile's childhood was very rough, and he always worried about Oliver dealing with the same issues. I guess you could say that he was a little overprotective."

"That must have been hard on Oliver. Was he resentful of his father?" Blu looked back at Hilda.

"Why are you asking me all of these questions?" Hilda studied Blu. "If you think my son had anything to do with this you are absolutely wrong. He's a good boy and he loved his father. He would never do anything to hurt Emile."

"I'm sorry if I upset you. I didn't mean to infer anything like that."

"I should hope not." She sighed. "I'm exhausted by all of this. I think I need to go rest."

"Of course you do. I'm sorry to have disturbed you. I'll see myself out."

"Wait just a minute. Blu, you said it was?"

"Yes." Blu turned back to face her.

"I want you to know something about my family, Blu. We might not be perfect, but we love one another in a way that most never get the chance to. Did Emile and Oliver fight? Of course they did. But they were always looking out for what was best for one another. Maybe they could have been kinder, but in the end there's no doubt in my mind that they both knew that they were loved by the other."

"I understand." Blu met her eyes. "I'm very sorry for your loss, Hilda. I hope that you and Oliver are able to get through this difficult time."

"We will. We still have each other."

Blu left the house with a sense of guilt that weighed on her shoulders. Had she been so caught up in the idea of an investigation that she forgot there were human hearts and lives involved in all of it?

CHAPTER 9

After leaving the Grovers' house, Blu decided to take a run along the beach. Usually an early morning activity for her, running always helped to clear her mind.

She stopped by the house to change. The empty driveway indicated that Rachel and the kids were still out. She changed into some running shorts and a top.

As she left the house again her cell phone rang. When she saw that it was AJ, her heart skipped a beat. She thought for a moment about not answering. She wanted to get used to distancing herself from him. But just when the call was about to go to voicemail, she picked up the phone.

"Hi, AJ."

"Hey, Blu. Am I interrupting something?"

"I was just going to go out for a run."

"Oh? Do you want some company?"

Blu looked down at her outfit. It was not exactly the most flattering thing to be seen in. She thought about how sweaty she would be when she finished running. Did she really want AJ to see her like that? Then it struck her. It shouldn't matter. If she was going to let go of him when summer was over, then why should she worry about how she looked? This would be a good test of her resolve.

"Sure."

"I can be there in about ten minutes."

"I'll wait for you." Those words caught in her throat. She spoke them on impulse but they felt so weighted once they were spoken.

"Good." AJ's voice softened. "I'll be there soon."

Blu took the time to stretch. Even though she hadn't begun to run yet, her heart raced and her breath was uneven.

When AJ appeared before her, she regretted her choice to run with him. He wore a sleeveless snug t-shirt that accentuated every ripple and rise of his chest.

She felt her cheeks grow hot as she looked away from him.

"Ready to run?"

"Sure." He smiled at her. "Thanks for letting me join in."

"Oh, it's fine. I've been a bit busy lately and haven't been getting my runs in. I'm way overdue. Why did you call in the first place?"

"Oh, right. I was just going to talk to you a bit about the plan for tonight."

"Is there a plan?"

"To be honest with you, the bar is going to be packed. I doubt there will be much time or room for you to be able to get any information out of Oliver."

"I guess I'll just have to try. Maddie is planning on joining me, so maybe she'll be able to get more out of him than I could."

AJ raised an eyebrow. "Did you run that past my uncle?"

"I didn't think I needed to." Blu met his eyes. "What's the difference?"

"I don't think there is one. He might just prefer to know."

"I'll tell him." Blu walked out across the sand.

AJ matched her pace. "So you're definitely going to be there tonight?"

"Yes."

AJ frowned. "I don't know if it's such a good idea to involve you in all of this."

"AJ, your uncle asked me for a reason. He trusts my instincts."

"Yes, and I'm sure he also likes the fact that you're not on his payroll so he won't be held responsible for anything that happens."

"Wow. That's a dark thought. Do you really think he would put me in danger?" Blu searched his eyes.

"No. I'm sorry, I don't. I just think that since he's got this idea in his head that you can help out with his cases, he's not being as cautious as he should be."

"Or as cautious as you think he should be?" Blu smiled at him. "Is it the fact that Oliver is a suspect in his father's death, or the fact that I'll be doing my very best to get information out of him?"

"Hm?" AJ turned to face her. "What are you trying to say, Blu?"

When he fixed his eyes on her directly Blu didn't feel as confident as she had a moment before. Was she really bold enough to say what she was thinking?

"Uh, well—just that maybe you might be just a little tiny bit jealous." Every bit of breath left Blu's body as she waited for his reaction.

He was silent for a long moment as he stared into her eyes.

"No, I'm sorry, Blu, but you're wrong about that."

Blu flushed and looked away.

In the next moment his arm wrapped around her waist and he pulled her close.

Blu met his eyes with surprise.

"I'm not just a little tiny bit jealous. I'm incredibly, unreasonably jealous. You should be getting *me* drunk, not Oliver."

Blu laughed as he wiggled his eyebrows. Her laughter was silenced by the soft warm pressure of his lips against the curve of her cheek. When he released her she could barely look at him.

"I don't imagine you're easy to get drunk."

"No. I'm not. But I don't imagine you'd need to get

me drunk." He grinned. "So are we going to run or what?"

"Oh yes!" Blu took off across the sand.

She needed to run to get all of her nerves to calm down. AJ's presence, as always, had stirred up every confusing sensation within her. Even through she ran as fast as she could, AJ easily matched her pace.

CHAPTER 10

The sand flew out from beneath Blu's feet as the balmy air sailed across her skin. Even with AJ at her side she began to relax. The sun, the sand, and the thrash of her heartbeat all worked together to ease her anxiety as she ran. She could hear AJ's ragged breath as he did his best to keep up.

By the time they reached an isolated section of the beach Blu was winded. She stopped and rested her hands on her knees.

"Whew." AJ plopped down on the sand. "Are you trying to kill me, woman?"

Blu laughed and sprawled out on the sand beside him. "I'm sorry. I don't usually run like that, but I needed to clear my head."

"About Emile?"

"Yes." Blu wiped a hand across her forehead. "I visited his wife today and—I don't know—something just felt off."

"She wasn't upset?"

"She was very upset. But she also said her husband

was likely having an affair."

"Ouch."

"Yeah." Blu sat up and looked over at AJ. "She mentioned it didn't bother her too much because most men have affairs."

AJ stared up at her. "You don't believe that, do you?"

"I don't know. I think Rachel worries about it with Marshall since he's gone so much."

"That doesn't mean he's cheating."

"You're right." Blu sighed and glanced out over the water.

AJ wrapped a hand around hers.

When she looked back at him he held her gaze.

"I would never do that. If I'm with someone, I'm with them one hundred percent."

"That's very noble of you."

"I think the only men who cheat are the men who don't know what it's like to be in love, Blu. Because once you fall in love, once you find that one person who you connect with on that deep level, there is no one else on earth that will satisfy you."

Blu smiled. "That sounds sweet."

"It's the truth." He trailed a fingertip along the tender skin of her palm. "It's what I believe."

"And how many times have you fallen in love, AJ?"

He met her eyes again. This time his cheeks reddened as he looked at her. "Just once."

Blu glanced away from him. Her heart fluttered. She

didn't want to believe that he meant her, but he certainly wasn't giving her any other explanation for his words. Still, she forced the thought out of her mind.

"I don't know what to think about love."

"That's the thing, Blu." He sat up beside her and gave her hand a light squeeze. "Love isn't about thinking. It's all about feeling."

"Well, if that's the case then maybe Hilda was right. Maybe she could feel that her husband didn't really love her. Maybe that's why it's so easy for her to believe that his lover killed him."

AJ smiled a little and released her hand. "I guess we'll find out more from Oliver tonight—I mean, if you do your job well." He winked at her.

"Are you doubting my ability to flirt, AJ?" Blu batted her eyes.

"Oh, yes." He laughed. "Very much."

"Thanks a lot." She playfully glared at him.

"I guess we'll find out tonight, hm?"

"I guess." Blu got to her feet. "Thanks for the run."

"I'd love to do it again sometime."

Blu smiled. "We'll see. You had a pretty hard time keeping up."

"I'll train harder." He winked, then jogged off across the sand.

Blu walked back toward the beach house to shower and change. As she approached the path that led to the house she caught sight of the lighthouse in the distance.

Maybe she wasn't skilled at flirting, but if it meant she could find out the truth about Emile's death, she would give it her best shot.

After showering, Blu chose an outfit that she wouldn't normally wear—a tank top paired with a skirt that was on the shorter side. She pulled her hair up into a perky ponytail and applied some rare-for-her lipstick. When she looked in the mirror she was a little startled. She looked a few years younger. With one more check of her outfit she headed out the door.

In the driveway, she sent a text to Maddie.

Are you ready?

A moment later she received a text in return.

Can't go after all. You're on your own!

Blu stared at the text. Without Maddie by her side, she wasn't sure that she'd be able to get any information out of Oliver.

With a sigh, she got into the car. Even if she was on her own, she had to give it a try.

The Beach Bum parking lot was so full that there was nowhere for Blu to park. She parked next door in a car wash that was closed for the night.

The sound of the music inside the bar drew her right to the door. When she opened the door, the scent of alcohol and nachos smacked her senses. She took a breath and walked further into the bar. The tables were full and every bar stool was occupied. Blu had never seen the Beach Bum so full. Whether it was for the special on beer or to show support for a local businessman, the night was looking to be quite a success already.

AJ seemed to have the attention of everyone at the bar as he went through one of his flashy bottle spinning rituals. Blu paused at the edge of the bar and watched with a smile. When AJ caught sight of her, the bottle slipped out of his hand and crashed into one of the large aluminum sinks. The bar erupted with laughter and mocking cheers.

Blu's cheeks grew hot as AJ met her eyes.

He grabbed the bottle out of the sink and began pouring shots for the people at the bar.

CHAPTER 11

Blu scanned the faces in the bar in search of Oliver. She recognized a few of the locals, but the bar was filled with many unfamiliar people. It occurred to her that Oliver might not even show up.

"He's not here yet." AJ set a beer down in front of her.

Blu smiled politely, but she had no intention of drinking the beer. "I'll have to keep my eyes peeled in this crowd."

"Yes, I expected we'd be busy, but this is a bit much. I've been trying to keep a head count to make sure we don't go over capacity."

"It's good for the family."

"I suppose." AJ held her gaze. "But things can easily get out of hand in a crowd like this. Just be careful Blu, alright? You may have your eye on Oliver, but I'm going to have my eyes on you."

"That sounds good to me. Just try not to drop any more bottles."

"No promises." He smiled so wide that his eyes

crinkled at the edges.

Blu pretended that her heart didn't skip a beat at the sight of that smile. Before she could say another word the door to the bar swung open. She recognized Oliver right away despite the baseball cap that he wore pulled down over his forehead.

As he walked up to the bar, Blu nodded to AJ. AJ nodded in return.

Blu picked up the bottle of beer that AJ had set down in front of her and walked toward Oliver.

"Oliver, right? I'm sure you don't remember me."

He looked at her from under the brim of his hat. "I remember."

"This is for you." She held out the bottle of beer to him.

"Thanks." He reached out to take it.

Blu pulled it back. "Wait a minute. Are you old enough to drink this?"

Oliver frowned. "I'm twenty-one. Do you want my ID?"

"No, that's okay." Blu smiled. "It's all yours."

As Oliver took the beer she wondered about how nervous he was. His hand shook as he gripped the bottle and his forehead was beaded with sweat.

"Thanks for this."

"I'm sorry about your father, Oliver."

"I know, I know. Everyone's sorry." Oliver tightened his grasp on the beer. "But it doesn't change anything, does it? All of the sorry in the world doesn't bring him back."

"No, you're right about that."

"I just keep thinking about the last time I saw him. It was so uneventful. He tossed me the keys to the cart and asked me to take over for the day. How is that for a goodbye?"

"It is a tough thing to go through, Oliver. Do you have anyone close that you can lean on? Someone that you can trust?"

"Just my mother." Oliver took a swig from the bottle of beer.

"No one else? It might be hard for her to comfort you while she's dealing with her own loss."

"We take care of each other."

"I'm sure that you do." Blu noticed a table had opened up. "Do you want to sit?"

"Sure." He followed her over to the table.

Blu sat down and tugged at the hem of her skirt. It was shorter than she'd anticipated.

Oliver sat down across from her.

"I wasn't sure if you would come here tonight."

"Well, it was nice of them to do this, you know. It would have meant a lot to my dad. He wasn't much of a drinker, but he was always talking about the local business owners and how they were all on the same footing. Everybody relies on tourism, and everybody struggles to get through the off season." He shrugged and took a drink of the beer. When he set the bottle down he looked up into Blu's eyes. "And I didn't know where else to go, really."

"You didn't want to be home with your mom?"

"My mom?" Oliver shook his head. "No. We might be close but this we can't go through together."

"It can be hard to be around someone when you're both grieving."

"Is she, though?" Oliver sighed and drank some more of the beer.

Blu reached out and touched the back of his free hand. It was strange for her to caress someone so casually, but Oliver's eyes fluttered with appreciation.

He sighed and sank back in his chair. "All they ever did was fight. I grew up thinking that was love—that was marriage—people being angry at one another all the time. Don't get me wrong, I love my mother. She's always taken care of me and looked out for me. I loved my father too. They are just very different people, and they couldn't ever seem to get along."

"They had been together a long time." Blu made a note in the back of her mind that Oliver's story about Emile's relationship with Hilda was different than Hilda's.

"Sure. I guess." He rubbed a hand along his forehead. "I asked my dad once why he stayed with her if all they did was fight. He looked at me and told me to grow up—that life wasn't about being happy. It was about making the best choices you could. I still don't know what he meant by that, but it's kind of heartbreaking to think he died without being happy."

"I'm sorry, that's hard advice to take. If it helps, I don't really agree with him. I think life is about being happy. I mean, other things too, but happiness is important."

He stared at his beer bottle. "Maybe. It doesn't matter now. Not for him."

Blu looked at him intently.

CHAPTER 12

"What about for you?" Blu curved her hand around Oliver's and held it. "Is there anything or anyone in your life that makes you happy?"

An instant smile lit up his face. He nodded. Whatever he held back earlier he was ready to share.

"One person."

"Oh? A girlfriend?" Blu smiled at him. "That doesn't surprise me."

"She's more than a girlfriend. I think she's the one, you know?" He looked into her eyes. "I can't ever stop thinking about her."

Blu's eyes narrowed slightly. She was sure that the person he spoke of was the same woman she'd seen at the lighthouse.

"You're lucky to have found her then. But where is she tonight? Is she going to meet you?"

"No." He cleared his throat and pulled his hand free of Blu's. "She's not going to be here. We keep things pretty much under the radar."

"Why is that?"

Oliver rolled his eyes. "My dad had some very traditional views on things."

"So he didn't like her?" Blu's heart sped up. That was even more reason to suspect the girlfriend.

"He didn't even know her. Not really. He never gave her the chance."

"It sounds like you really care about this girl. What was her name again?" Blu lifted an eyebrow.

"Marta. Her name is Marta. I guess that's the one good thing that came out of this. Now we'll be able to be together."

"Marta? Have you known her long?"

"We were in high school together." He smiled. "We knew from the first moment that we saw each other that we were in love." He pulled out his wallet and opened it up. "Isn't she beautiful?"

Blu stared at the photograph, which was almost identical to the sketch. Marta most certainly was the woman that Blu had seen in the lighthouse. "Gorgeous. You're one lucky guy, Oliver."

"I think so. I just hope she feels the same. She hasn't been returning my calls today." He shook his head. "I know things are a little crazy, and that's probably all it is, but I just wish she would answer the phone."

Blu bit into her bottom lip. She was tempted to tell him that Marta wasn't calling him back because she was the one who murdered his father. But when she looked into his forlorn gaze she couldn't imagine making things worse for him.

"I'm sure she'll call soon."

He nodded. "I probably sound pretty pathetic to you, huh?"

"Not at all. Why would you think that?"

"Well, here you are, this beautiful woman sharing a drink with me, and all I can talk about is my girlfriend."

Blu blushed at the comment. "That doesn't sound pathetic at all to me. I think it's sweet. You must really care about her."

"I do." He fiddled with his beer bottle. "She's been through a lot."

"Life isn't always easy."

"No." He frowned. "No, it's not." He finished his beer. "I think you're right, though. I should be home with my mother. She shouldn't be alone after something like this."

"It would be good for you to be there for her."

"I guess with just the two of us left, we're going to have to figure out what to do next."

"I'll walk you out, alright?"

"Thanks." He stood up and glanced around the packed bar. "I have to say that it's good to know that all these people would come out in support of my father and my family. It means a lot."

"You have a good solid community around you, Oliver. Don't be afraid to lean on it for support."

He nodded and wrapped his arm around hers as they

walked toward the door. "You've been so kind to me, Blu." He leaned in close and spoke quietly in her ear. "Thank you."

"You're welcome." Blu gave his arm a little squeeze.

When she looked toward the door she caught sight of AJ watching them. A pang of guilt caused her muscles to tense. It was silly. AJ was a friend, and she'd done nothing wrong, yet she couldn't bring herself to look him in the eye as she left the bar on Oliver's arm.

Blu walked Oliver to his car. After their conversation, she suspected that he might go to see his girlfriend instead of his mother.

Once he started his engine, Blu walked to her car. She thought about going back inside to speak to AJ, but she knew he was busy. She wanted to see where Oliver would go. Since she was parked on the road it was easy for her to slide out behind Oliver's car and follow him.

He drove in a familiar direction. It didn't take long for Blu to realize that he was actually driving toward his mother's house. Blu parked a few houses down, close enough to see him, but far enough not to be noticed.

She watched as Oliver walked up to the front door of his mother's house. She saw a light come on in the upstairs bedroom. Then, as Oliver opened the door, she saw a shadowy figure climb right out of the second floor window. He climbed down the trellis and jumped to the ground right after Oliver stepped inside.

Blu jumped out of the car in an attempt to get a good

look at who he was, but he ran across the backyard and disappeared.

As she got back into her car it dawned on her that maybe Emile wasn't the only one who was hadn't been faithful in his marriage.

She drove back to the beach house with a lot on her mind. If Marta really was the killer then would it even matter that Hilda was seeing someone else? If she revealed that Hilda had someone in her bedroom, would Oliver's life be even more damaged? How did a young man recover from losing his father, his girlfriend, and his mother all in the course of one investigation?

CHAPTER 13

Blu cut the headlights on her car before she pulled into the driveway of the beach house. She didn't want to wake the family, likely sound asleep inside. She made her way quietly to the door. She slid the key into the lock on the door. Just as she was about to turn it, she heard someone step up beside her.

With a gasp she spun around and looked right into Chief Pitman's eyes.

"Don't do that!" She smacked him hard on the chest. Only after her hand made contact did she realize that it might not have been the best idea to hit the chief of police.

"I'm sorry." He adjusted his hat. "I didn't mean to sneak up on you. I wanted to speak with you and I figured that the kids might be sleeping, so I didn't want to call out."

"I'm sorry for hitting you." She frowned.

"It's okay. I won't arrest you. This time." He smirked. "So do you have an update for me? AJ said you were cozied up with the kid—with Oliver—most of the night."

"We were not cozied up together. But I did talk to him. I have the name of his girlfriend. I saw her picture. It's the same woman that I saw at the lighthouse. Her name is Marta."

"No last name?"

"No, sorry."

"That's not much to go on." He shook his head. "Are you sure that it was the same girl?"

"I'm sure. Also, he mentioned that his father and mother fought a lot. Hilda also told me that she suspected Emile was having an affair." Blu bit into her bottom lip, holding back the information about what she'd witnessed after following Oliver.

"Wait a minute, when did you talk to Hilda?"

"I went to see her today."

"Why didn't you tell me?" Chief Pitman crossed his arms.

"I didn't think it was important. I just wanted to get a better idea of Emile's family."

"You should have told me."

"What's the difference? You asked me to get information out of Oliver tonight."

"I asked you. You agreed. Instead of giving me the heads-up about your conversation with Hilda, you went off on your own."

"I still don't see what the problem is." Blu frowned.

"If we're going to work together, I need to be able to trust you, Blu. I can't trust you if you're going to go behind my back to do things."

"It wasn't behind your back. I just didn't know that you would want to be notified. I didn't mean any disrespect."

"From now on, if you're going to go off and conduct your own interviews, I want you to tell me. This case is important to me. I don't want any mistakes. Understand?"

"Yes." Again Blu considered mentioning the man she saw climb out of Hilda's window. But after thinking about the look in Oliver's eyes she just couldn't do it. Marta was clearly the main, if not the only suspect, so why bring up Hilda's lover? He likely had nothing to do with the crime. She brought her attention back to the chief, who seemed to be waiting for more from her. "Good night, Chief Pitman."

"Good night, Blu. Thank you for your help."

"You're welcome."

Blu stepped inside and closed the door behind her. She crept to her room and sat down on the edge of her bed. For a moment she toyed with her phone as she considered calling AJ. "He's probably still closing up the bar."

Blu stretched out on the bed. She closed her eyes. No matter how much she tried to distract herself, she couldn't shake the memory of the way AJ had looked at her as she left the bar. She wondered how long she could go on pretending that she wasn't absolutely enamored with him. He'd made his feelings very clear, but Blu couldn't risk getting her emotions tangled up in what would only be a summer affair.

While she prepared breakfast the next morning, Blu sent a text to Maddie.

Marley's hair is almost fixed, it's just a little pink. Would you like to meet at the playground this morning?

She turned and served the kids eggs and toast.

"I want pizza!" Marley frowned.

"Oh, that sounds good." Joey nodded.

"Not for breakfast." Blu grinned. "How about we get pizza for lunch? Does that sound good?"

"Yes!" Marley grinned.

"Great." Blu glanced at her phone to see that Maddie had texted back.

We'll meet you there.

Blu smiled. She could use some advice from Maddie, and after their being cooped up in a hair salon the day before she was sure the kids could use some outdoor activity.

After breakfast they drove to the park near the beach. The moment they parked, the kids ran for the playground. Blu waved to Maddie, who waited on one of the benches.

"You beat us here."

"I couldn't wait to find out what happened last night." Maddie smiled up at her. "So, dish."

CHAPTER 14

Blu sat down beside Maddie on the park bench.

"Well, to be honest, I didn't find out too much. Oliver's girlfriend is named Marta, and I'm pretty sure his mother is having an affair. Apparently that wasn't quite as much as Chief Pitman expected."

"Well, Marta isn't much to go on."

"I know that. But it was more than he had." Blu frowned and crossed her arms.

"Are you sure that he didn't tell you anything else about her? A place they liked to go? How they met?"

"Oh, well he did say they met in high school."

"There it is! That's the only clue that you need." Maddie grinned and pulled out her phone. "Let's see, do you have an idea of where Oliver went to school?"

"I saw a picture of him in a soccer uniform. Caldero Wildcats."

"Okay, Caldero High School is one of the local schools. Give me a second." Maddie tapped away on the keyboard on her phone.

Blu watched as Joey swung as high as he could on the swing.

"Okay, I've got Oliver. Give me another second." She skimmed through her phone. "Here we go. Marta Milagros. There's even a picture of them together. See?" She held up the phone, which displayed a photograph of Oliver and Marta. They sat together on a bench and smiled at the camera.

"Yes, that's her. You're amazing, Maddie!"

"I'm happy I could do something for you considering what happened to Marley's hair."

"Maddie, I told you that's not your fault. Let it go."

"Still. At least we found Marta. Are you going to tell Chief Pitman?"

Blu watched as Marley raced across the playground to beat her brother to the slide. She thought about the innocent smile on Marta's lips and the glow in Oliver's eyes when he spoke of her.

"I will." She cleared her throat. "I just might take a peek at her myself first."

"I can find you her current address." Maddie tapped on her phone again. "I'm texting it to you."

"How can you do all of that?"

"I've got skills!" Maddie grinned. "I might also have a bit of a social media addiction." She cringed. "But Blu, if you've already got Chief Pitman concerned about you, you should think about being honest with him."

"It's not that I don't trust him. It's just that he doesn't

have a gentle bone in his body."

"That you know of." Maddie raised an eyebrow.

"What do you mean?"

"Well, look at AJ. He's pretty considerate and kind, don't you think?"

"Yes." Blu tried to hide the automatic smile that curved her lips the moment AJ's name was mentioned.

"He had to learn that from somewhere. I get the impression that Chief Pitman plays a fatherly role in his life."

"That's a good point." Blu frowned. "But AJ can be pretty intense too, just like his uncle. I just want a chance to figure out who Marta is and how she might be involved. It's not like I'm hiding anything. He had the same information that I gave you, so I'm sure he'll figure out who Marta is on his own."

"If you say so. I trust that you know what you're doing. But if you want Chief Pitman to trust you, then you should think about giving him a reason to."

"Listen to you." Blu sighed. "Getting all wise on me."

"What can I say? Being a nanny has made me realize just how dangerous this world can be."

"Good point." Blu nodded. "Speaking of dangerous, Brennan looks like he's not enjoying himself too much."

"Moody cannot even begin to describe that boy lately."

"Maybe he needs a sport or something?"

"He's very anti-sport. I think I'm going to take them

to the skating rink later. Maybe that will make him crack a smile."

"I hope so. Let me know how it goes."

"Maybe you should bring the kids. You could invite AJ."

"Skating?"

"It's the perfect opportunity to fake a fall and end up in his arms." Maddie wiggled her eyebrows.

"Ah, there went the good advice."

"I'm serious. Summer isn't going to last forever, Blu."

"That's exactly why we need to stay friends." Blu narrowed her eyes. "What's the point of starting a relationship that can't last?"

"Look, you can be as logical as you want, but I promise you, if the summer ends before you have the chance to kiss that man, you're going to regret it for the rest of your life." She typed out a message on her phone.

"That's a bit dramatic, don't you think?"

Maddie looked into her eyes. "I don't know. Is it?"

Blu frowned. "Let's go, kids, time to go."

"Uh huh." Maddie smirked. "If you want to meet us for skating later we'll be there around two."

"Fine, but I'm not inviting AJ."

"Oh—oops." Maddie looked up from her phone. "I might have already done that."

"Maddie!"

"What?" She widened her eyes, then grinned. "Someone has to look out for you."

"Apparently." Blu shook her head and steered the kids toward the car.

"Love you, Blu!" Maddie called out, teasing her.

Blu laughed. "Yeah. Love you too, girl."

Once in the car, Blu opened the GPS in her phone. She retrieved the address that Maddie had texted her, typed it in, and waited for the map to generate.

"We're just going to take a little detour, kids, then we'll hit the pizza place for lunch."

"A detour where?" Joey tried to peek at the map.

"Nowhere important. We're not going to stop, we're just going to drive around a bit."

Blu started the car and pulled out onto the road. She cranked up the children's radio station and smiled as the kids sang along. She was about halfway to her destination when a patrol car pulled up behind her.

She glanced in the rearview mirror at it, then at her speedometer. She was well within the speed limit. Confident that she wouldn't be pulled over, she smiled at the kids. A moment later flashing lights and sirens alerted her to the fact that she was indeed going to be pulled over.

She sighed and steered the car off to the side of the road.

"Blu, what is it? Were you speeding?"

"No. It's nothing, I'm sure. Just relax, Joey."

"Copper!" Marley giggled.

"Sh, Marley!" Blu took a deep breath and reached for

her insurance information.

"Where are you going, Blu?" Chief Pitman rested his hands on the doorframe.

"Chief Pitman? Are you following me?"

"Possibly. I figured out who Marta is. I was going to head out to her house to speak with her. Much to my surprise I find myself driving behind your vehicle, and I have the intuition that we're going to the same place." The chief looked with narrowed eyes at what must have been her guilty expression. "So how did you get her address? Did you have it all along?"

"No, I didn't. My friend Maddie was able to find it all on the Internet. I was going to tell you."

"Right. After you questioned her?"

"I was just going to drive past and see if I could catch a glimpse of her. "

"Then I'm glad that I stopped you. Blu, you may know the beach pretty well, but you know nothing about the neighborhoods further away. This woman lives in one of the roughest neighborhoods in the area. You would have put yourself and these two kids in danger."

"Oh, I didn't realize that." Blu frowned.

"A GPS can't tell you the crime rate. That's why we're supposed to be a team. Are you going to be on my team or are we going to be on different sides?"

Blu grimaced as she glanced in the rearview mirror. The very thought of putting the kids in danger made her sick to her stomach.

"We're a team. I'm sorry, Chief Pitman."

"Good. Then take the kids home. I'll let you know what I find out. Okay?"

"Okay."

Blu waited until Chief Pitman was back in the patrol car, then she turned her car around.

As she drove back toward the beach, she realized that even though she considered herself a good investigator, there were some things that she didn't think through. She needed to be more careful when the kids were in her care.

CHAPTER 15

Blu drove back toward the beach. One glance in the back seat told her that the kids were still a bit shaken by being pulled over. She decided it was time to brighten their mood.

"Pizza time!"

She turned down the road that led to the pizza place. The kids began to chant their desire for pizza. Blu pulled into the parking lot and was about to park when she noticed that the pizza place was not open.

"Pizza, pizza, pizza!" Joey and Marley chanted.

Blu gulped as she realized that it was the only pizza place she knew of. She thought about doing a search for one, but after what happened with Marta's address she didn't want to risk it. However, if she didn't get some pizza in front of the two kids in her back seat she was fairly certain that she would be in quite a bit of danger.

After a moment she dialed AJ's number.

"Well, hello there, I thought maybe you lost my num—"

"—No time for that, AJ. I need to find a pizza place."

"Vincenzo's is great."

"I agree, but it's also closed. I was hoping that you might know of another place."

"I might."

Blu could barely hear him over the demands for pizza coming from the back seat. "AJ, please, the kids are ready to chew through the interior."

"Okay, I'll tell you about my favorite pizza place—it's only for locals, not for tourists, but you have to promise me one thing."

"What?" She was quite enjoying his teasing.

"I get to join you for lunch."

Blu smiled at the thought. "Alright, I guess I can promise that."

"Great. I'll text you the address and meet you there."

"Thanks, AJ."

Blu hung up the phone. An instant later the address came through. Blu drove the few blocks to it. If it weren't for AJ's directions, she never would have found it. The pizza place was a tiny shop in a strip mall, it only had two tables inside.

"Hello?"

"Hi there." A man stepped out of the back room. "How can I help you?"

"One large cheese pizza and garlic knots please."

"Okay, it will be ready in about ten minutes." He smiled and winked at the kids.

Right after Blu got the kids settled at one of the

tables, the door to the pizza shop swung open. Blu looked up to see AJ's thick frame filling the doorway. She smiled without meaning to and when he smiled back she blushed.

"My hero."

"If all it takes is a pizza place, then I'm getting off easy."

"You have no idea what it's like to be held hostage by two hungry children. Trust me, you're my hero." Blu sat down at the table.

AJ sat down across from her and looked at the kids. "Well, you two are in for a treat. This is the best pizza in the state."

"Really?" Blu glanced over her shoulder at the menu on the wall. "I've never heard of it."

"When you live in a tourist town, you learn to keep the best local places a secret, otherwise you'll never get a chance to eat the food. If this place was flooded with tourists, then they'd have to expand, raise prices, change their menus, hire new help, and by next year it wouldn't even be recognizable."

"I've never thought about it that way." Blu smiled at the man in a white apron who brought out their pizza. "Wait! Joey, it's hot." She shooed away his hand as he reached for a slice.

"I'll do that." The man smiled and served them each a slice on a paper plate.

"Thank you." Blu grabbed Marley's plate to cut up

the pizza.

"So I heard you had a run-in with my uncle this morning."

"You did?"

"Yes. Let's just say he called me to tell me what you did."

"I don't understand. Why would he call you?"

"Because he was worried about you, Blu. And I guess he thinks that I might be able to get through to you."

"I'm not sure I'm comfortable with the two of you talking about me."

"I don't blame you." AJ smiled. "That's why I'm here with you, not lecturing you about how dangerous your little field trip was today."

"That sounds a little like a lecture."

"It's just conversation."

Blu handed Marley back her pizza. "Look, I respect your uncle but he's not exactly delicate. The way Oliver described Marta was so sweet. I just wanted a chance to get a glimpse of her. I mean Oliver just lost his father, I didn't want him to lose his girlfriend too—not if he didn't need to."

"Well, that's very thoughtful of you, but did you ever consider that Marta and Oliver might have planned the whole thing?"

Blu blinked. She stared down at her slice of pizza. "Not really."

"Or you just don't want to think it?"

"Maybe." She glanced up at him. "I know Marta was there. I saw her run past me."

"And you know that Oliver was there. It's rather convenient that he would be fully visible at his hot dog cart while Marta took care of their problem."

"But was he a problem?"

"Maybe Oliver didn't want to wait to inherit the family business."

"A hot dog cart?" Blu shook her head. "No. Oliver said that Emile was having money problems. There wouldn't be much to inherit."

"That's what Oliver told you." AJ leaned across the table and met her eyes. "Con artists come in all shapes and sizes, Blu. I saw the way he spoke to you last night. I saw how he had you wrapped around his finger, dangling on his every word."

CHAPTER 16

Blu stared at AJ with a quirked eyebrow. "I'm sorry? You saw all of that? Because all I saw was a grieving son who was struggling with his loss. I think you got the wrong impression, AJ, and I don't appreciate what you're implying."

AJ frowned and glanced over at the kids, who were fighting over a garlic knot. "I didn't mean to imply anything. I guess I just want to be sure that you're keeping a clear head about all this."

"Joey, share it with your sister." Blu turned her attention back to AJ. "It's your uncle's job to follow the facts of the case. But I trust my instincts. Maybe Oliver is a con artist like you think, but I don't think he's a killer."

"Maybe not. But maybe his girlfriend is."

"Do you know something that I don't?"

"My uncle did some research on Marta's family. They've been involved in organized crime. In fact several of her relatives still are."

"Seriously?" Blu raised an eyebrow. "That's unexpected."

"You see?" He held her gaze. "This case is going to get dangerous fast. I just want you to exercise some caution."

"I will." Blu nodded. "From now on, I will."

AJ focused on his slice of pizza for a moment, then he cleared his throat. "So I got this strange text from Maddie."

Blu pressed the heel of her palm to her forehead. "I know, I'm sorry."

"Why? I enjoy roller-skating."

"You do?"

He grinned. "I need a rematch. You ran me ragged on the sand yesterday. Let's see if I can skate circles around you. Hm? Are you going to be there?"

Blu gritted her teeth. She could imagine how embarrassing it would be when she fell flat on her rear in front of AJ.

"I'm not a very good skater."

"Oh? I can teach you."

"Are we going roller-skating with Brennan? I want to go Blu, please!" said Joey.

"Alright, alright." Blu laughed. "I'll give it a try. But I'm warning you, I'm going to spend more time on the floor than I am on my skates."

"Not with me around to catch you." AJ smiled as he took his last bite of pizza.

Blu smiled across the table at him. His confident nature was infectious.

"That could be fun."

"It will be. You need a break from all this, and the kids need a fun afternoon."

"I guess you're right. We'll meet you there."

"Perfect."

After they left the pizza place, Blu and the kids spent some time at the beach. As she watched the kids build sandcastles she felt a subtle flutter in her chest. Their youth shielded them from what the rest of the world couldn't ignore. Life was hard at times and impossible at others.

Her thoughts returned to the fact that Emile had been faced with financial difficulties. How desperate was he? He had lied to his son about where he was. He had lied to his wife about the company he kept. Would it be so much of a stretch to think that rather than securing a legal loan he'd possibly gotten himself involved with a loan shark?

If that was the case, then perhaps Marta wasn't innocent at all. Perhaps she had been at that lighthouse to do business for her family. Oliver might not have even known that Marta was there.

She pulled out her phone and thumbed through the notes she'd made about the case. Not once had Oliver mentioned that he knew Marta was there at the lighthouse.

As she watched the children play, she dialed Oliver's

number. It rang three times before he answered.

"Hello?"

"Hi, Oliver. It's Blu."

"Oh. Hi."

"Are you busy right now?"

"Not really."

"Oliver, I want to ask you a question and I'd appreciate it if you were honest with me."

"Okay, sure."

"Did you know that Marta was at the lighthouse? The day that your father died?"

"Yes. Of course I did. I mean, she was there with me."

"She was? Because you seemed pretty surprised when you saw the sketch of her."

"What?" He paused. "How did you know about that?"

"Just answer the question, Oliver."

"Look, Marta was there. I didn't identify her when I saw the sketch because with her family's history, I knew that the wrong assumptions would be made."

"I guess you didn't know that I saw her there? I'm the one who gave the information to make the sketch."

"No, I didn't know that. I wish you would have told me. Are you a cop or something?"

"No, I'm not a cop—just a nanny. Oliver, I'm not trying to cause you trouble. I want to help you and your father. But in order to do that you have to be honest with me."

"I am being honest with you. Marta was there because I was there—not for any other reason."

"She must have been to the top of that lighthouse plenty of times before. You don't think it was strange that she was at the top of the lighthouse with your father when you didn't even know that he was there?"

"What I think is strange is that my father is dead and you are calling me to harass me. I don't have anything to say to you. It's bad enough they arrested Marta. Now I'm going to have to figure out how to come up with bail money—all because of your sketch."

"She was there, Oliver. Whether you want to face the facts or not, she was there."

"Marta would not hurt my father."

"Not even if he owed a large debt to her family?"

"What are you talking about?"

Marley brought a shell over to Blu to add to her pile.

"I'm talking about Marta's family's connection to organized crime. Are you going to tell me that you've known her since high school and you didn't know about that?"

"I knew." He sighed. "I knew about her family. But that has nothing to do with her! Marta wasn't involved in any of that. She didn't want to be. She's a good person, and now thanks to you, she's behind bars."

"The only way to get to the truth is to tell the truth, Oliver. Think about that."

"Think about losing my number." He hung up the phone.

Blu cringed as she slid her phone back into her pocket. She hadn't gained much from the conversation.

"Thank you for the shells, Marley. They're beautiful."

"More?" Marley smiled.

"Tomorrow. Now we have to go get ready to roller-skate!"

"Yes!" Joey shouted.

CHAPTER 17

Blu drove the kids back to the beach house. They changed into clothes more suited for roller-skating. Blu took the time to put Marley's hair up into a ponytail. She wondered if she would be able to stay upright for any length of time.

When they left for the skating rink Blu sent Rachel a text to let her know where they'd be. The skating rink wasn't too far from the beach, but it was usually a popular destination only when it was a rainy day. Since the sun was shining brightly, the parking lot was rather empty. She noticed right away that AJ's jeep was not there. Maddie's car was.

She led the kids into the skating rink and paid for admission and skate rental. Then she began the difficult task of getting the skates on two wiggly excited children.

"Blu!" Maddie slammed into the side of the skating rink. "I'm so glad that you came!"

"We're here. I'm not sure how long we'll be on the rink." Blu smiled as she tightened the laces on Marley's skates.

"Chrissa is dying to teach Marley to skate. If you're okay with it she'll take her around the rink."

"Sure, that's fine with me." Blu smiled. "Joey's an old pro so I'm sure that he'll be chasing Brennan around the rink."

"Good luck." Maddie rolled her eyes. "Brennan spotted a few girls that he's trying to keep up with."

Blu helped the kids over to the rink.

"Oh, wait a minute, where are your skates?" Maddie grinned. "You don't think that you're getting out of this do you?"

"No, I don't." Blu grinned. "I just have to get them on." She tugged her skates on and tightened the laces as fast as she could. "No pictures!"

Maddie hid her cell phone in her pocket. "I don't know what you're talking about." She whistled.

"Uh huh, if I end up trending somewhere I know who to blame."

Maddie wiggled her eyebrows and helped Blu onto the rink. As soon as the wheels on the skates hit the slick floor, Blu began to wobble.

"Oh you weren't kidding." Maddie winced. "You're going to have to get used to them, I guess."

"Or I could just take them off and go sit down."

"No, I don't think that would be a good idea. Remember, your Prince Charming is going to be here any minute."

"Ha!"

"I'm serious. You don't want him to think that you chickened out."

Blu sighed. She knew that Maddie was right. AJ was nice enough to join her for the afternoon. She could at least make an effort.

"I'll be back, I'm going to check on Brennan and make sure he hasn't proposed to anyone!" Maddie spun right past her.

Blu clung to the side of the rink. Her feet wanted to go in two different directions. Her knees wobbled as she tried to get her balance.

"Blu, let's race!" Joey waved to her from the middle of the rink.

"I'll be there soon, Joey." Blu smiled and waved to him. She knew she would never get to the middle of the rink, but she didn't want to disappoint Joey. Marley and Chrissa whizzed past hand in hand. Blu sighed and shook her head.

"Wow, you are exactly where I left you." Maddie laughed as she skidded to a stop beside Blu.

"Oh yes, it's quite amusing. It will be even more amusing when I end up in the emergency room."

"See, that's the problem. You are too afraid to just let go and enjoy."

"If I let go, I'm going to land on my rear end, and trust me, that is not something that I'm going to enjoy."

"Just give it a try. Here, we'll go together." Maddie

held out her hand to her.

Blu glanced over the rest of the people in the skating rink. She didn't see AJ. "I don't think he's here yet sweetie," Maddie said. "But that doesn't mean that we can't have fun."

Blu nodded. "You're right." She took Maddie's hand. "Let's give this a try."

"Just take it easy. It's all in the hip and the knee. Once you get the feel for it, you'll never forget. Glide, glide, roll. See?" Maddie smiled. "Now we're flying."

Blu was surprised that it did feel quite a bit like she was flying. In fact, it was fun. For just a split second Blu forgot about Emile, Oliver, and Marta. But that moment was gone as fast as it came.

"Maddie, wait, it's too fast."

"Blu, you're doing great. We have to keep pace with the song."

Blu started to get dizzy as she watched the other skaters spin in circles around her. "Maddie, don't, I'm going to fall."

"What? I can't hear you. The music's too loud."

Blu swung her free arm in an attempt to catch her balance. The more she tried to gain her balance, the more off-balance she became. Her right foot flew up into the air in the same moment that her left foot rolled back behind her. She knew that she was about to hit the floor. Just as she began to tumble she felt a solid arm around her waist. When she looked toward the person who'd caught her she saw that it was AJ. He coasted her over to the side wall of the rink.

"I see you got started without me."

"If you can call that getting started." Blu laughed.

"Haven't you ever skated before?"

"Sure, but it was a long time ago."

AJ stared into her eyes. "Then we just need to refresh your memory. Here, you can stand right in front of me."

"I don't think I'm going to be standing at all." Blu looked at him nervously.

"Trust me, I'm not going to let you fall." He guided her in front of him.

At first Blu kept her footing. But the moment she tried to roll one foot forward her other foot tried to roll back the other way.

AJ's hands grasped her hips.

Her eyes widened.

"Relax. It's all in the hips. You have to relax." He grinned at her and she tried to focus on something other than his hands on her body.

CHAPTER 18

Blu closed her eyes for just a moment. Then she willed herself to relax. "I'll give it one more try." She placed her hands over AJ's to be sure that he didn't let her fall. Then she began to skate.

It only took a few strides before she and AJ were in perfect sync. The sensation was similar to soaring. With AJ close to her, she didn't even think about falling. Instead she could feel her muscles engaging the way that they were supposed to.

Before she realized it, they'd looped the rink three times. She only noticed how fast they were going when she began to get winded. AJ must have been worn out too, because he guided them both over to the edge of the rink.

"How was that?" He grinned. Only when Blu's hands were on the side of the rink did he let go of her hips. "Fun?"

"So much fun!" Blu grinned. "I don't think I've had that much fun in a long time."

"See? I'm a good influence, no matter what my uncle

says." He grinned.

"Hm." Blu winked at him. "I think I want to get something to drink, and I'd better check on the kids."

She noticed Joey and Brennan raced back and forth down the middle of the rink. Maddie, Chrissa, and Marley skated in one big group.

"I guess it's just us." AJ held his hand out to her.

Blu took his hand and leaned on the wall as well. Once on the carpeted floor her balance was better. They made their way to the concession section.

"What would you like? I'll get it."

"Just some water."

"Are you sure? No snacks?"

"No, thanks. Remember how much pizza I ate?" She smiled.

"Okay I'll be right back."

Blu settled in at one of the tables. There was a clear line of sight to the skating rink. But what drew her attention was a couple squabbling near the short hallway that led to an emergency exit. The woman's back was to her, and she didn't recognize the man, but from their posture and the man's expressions she knew that they were arguing.

"Blu!"

Blu turned to look at AJ.

"They have corn dogs!"

Blu's stomach flipped at the thought. "No, thanks." She shook her head.

He shrugged and turned back to the person behind the counter.

Blu caught sight of the couple again. The man put his hand on the woman's shoulder rather roughly. The woman lowered her head as her body shook. Every muscle in Blu's body tensed as she prepared to intervene if she needed to. She hated to see any kind of domestic violence, and she wasn't about to let it unfold with her in the building.

But when the woman turned away from the man, Blu froze with shock. It wasn't just any woman, it was Hilda, Emile's wife. Then it struck her that the man who stood behind her could easily be the man she'd seen climbing down the side of Hilda's house. If Hilda and this man were fighting, then she could be in danger.

"Here you go, Blu." AJ handed her a bottle of water. He held a can of soda and a corn dog in his other hand.

Blu glanced over at him. "Thank you."

"Is something wrong?" He followed her line of sight.

"It's Hilda and some guy. I think they're arguing. I don't know, it seems like he might hurt her."

"Well, let's put a stop to that." Without a moment's hesitation AJ put down his can of soda and the corn dog. With Blu right beside him he strode up to the couple.

"Hilda, are you okay? Is this guy harassing you?" Blu narrowed her eyes.

AJ folded his arms across his chest.

"No, I'm fine." Hilda looked at the guy, and Blu

thought she seemed less than fine. She turned back toward them. "Really, everything's okay."

"We were just having a conversation." The man looked between Blu and AJ. "It's none of your business."

"It's my business if you're treating her with disrespect. Hilda?" said Blu.

Hilda sniffled. "It's not his fault. It's me. We were just having a little argument—not the best place for it, I know."

"Why are you here?" Blu studied her. "Are you two skating together?"

"No. I came here because my son was supposed to be here. But he's not. So we should be going."

"Hilda, wait." Blu touched the crook of her arm. "Are you sure it's safe to leave with him?"

"Look, lady, you have the wrong idea." The man shook his head and gave Blu a hard look.

"Watch it." AJ locked eyes with him.

"Really, it's fine. Jack and I work together at the shop. With what's happened to Emile, our emotions are just running high. We're both fine and I feel perfectly safe with him."

Blu frowned. Hilda appeared to be telling the truth, but she had no way of knowing that for sure. "If you need me, Hilda, please call. I know this is a tough time for you."

"Yes, it is. I appreciate you wanting to help me, Blu, but it's really not what you think. We should be going.

Jack, come on." She tugged at the man's thick arm.

Blu watched as the two walked away.

MACI GRANT

CHAPTER 19

Blu felt AJ's hand curve along her shoulder as Hilda and Jack walked away.

"You okay?"

"Yes." Blu narrowed her eyes. "But something is not right there. I'm going to find out who he is."

"I know Jack. He comes into the bar now and then. He's worked with Hilda for quite some time."

"I have a feeling they're doing more than working."

"What makes you think that?" AJ looked over at her. His hand lingered on her shoulder.

"I'm pretty sure that I saw him climb out of her window last night."

"What?"

"I followed Oliver after he left the bar. I wanted to see if he would go to meet his girlfriend. Instead, he went home to his mother's house. When Oliver was at the front door I saw a man who looked a lot like Jack climbing out the second story window."

"Did you tell Uncle Paul?"

Blu bit into her bottom lip. She realized that leaving

out the tidbit of information might be seen as uncooperative.

"AJ, I just didn't want to risk exposing an affair if Hilda had nothing to do with the murder. Obviously she didn't. I mean, Marta was at the scene of the crime and with her family's history it's no surprise that she acted violently. What good would it do to reveal the truth about Hilda?"

AJ ran his hand back through his hair and pulled his other hand free of her shoulder. "You might be right about that, but I'm not sure Uncle Paul will see it that way. The thing is, you can't make assumptions.

Blu sighed. "I'm not sure. I think that Chief Pitman said that Hilda was at the shop the whole time."

"But who is her alibi? If it's Jack, then it might be flawed."

"You're right." Blu met his eyes. "I need to find out exactly what your uncle knows."

"Well, a good way to start is by telling him exactly what you know."

Blu smiled at his words. "Good point."

Maddie, Chrissa, and Marley skated over to the edge of the rink. "What's going on Blu? Is everything okay?" said Maddie.

"Yes, I think so. I need to get in touch with Chief Pitman. I hate to ask this, but do you think—"

"Sure I can." Maddie smiled.

"I'll help." AJ got back to his feet and joined them on

the rink.

"If they get worn out, we'll go back to my place. You just do what you need to do to get this case settled," said Maddie.

"Okay, I'll try."

Blu changed back into her sneakers. Then she placed a call to Chief Pitman.

"Blu, I have some news for you."

"I have some for you too."

"Let's meet then."

"At the station?"

"Outside the station. I want us to be able to speak freely. There's a nice courtyard right beside the building. Okay?"

"Alright, I'll meet you there."

"Thanks—and Blu?"

"Yes?"

"Be careful, there may be a lot more involved in this murder than either of us realized."

"I will." Blu hung up the phone. Her gaze shifted to the skating rink. She saw AJ, Maddie, and all of the kids skating together.

For a moment it struck her that she should be out there too. If it weren't for her journalistic nature, she would be. As much as the thought tugged at her heart, it also frightened her. She wasn't someone who could just ignore a crime. She had a deep need to find the truth. Even though she might have walked away from her career as a journalist, her desire to get to the bottom of things had not faded; and if she was being honest with herself, she was quite enjoying what had turned into a summer full of mysteries.

After she left the kids with Maddie, Blu drove to the police station. She was glad that Chief Pitman wanted to meet somewhere other than the interrogation room. She was quite certain that his temper would be tested by what she had to share with him.

In the courtyard by the side of the station, she saw that Chief Pitman was already waiting for her.

CHAPTER 20

Blu parked and walked toward Chief Pitman.

He turned to look at her with the type of squint that made her think of old western movies. He had a way of knowing that something was up no matter how hard she tried to hide it.

"Blu."

"Chief Pitman."

"What do you have to tell me?"

"I heard that you arrested Marta."

"Yes we did. We have a witness placing her at the scene of the crime, motive, and a criminal history. There was no reason not to arrest her."

"What about Oliver?"

"What about him?"

"He told me that she was there to see him."

"You and I both know that is not true."

"But if he claims it's the case it will contradict what you are saying happened."

"How so?" He settled his hands to his hips. "The

only thing that it will do is implicate Oliver. It will look as if he and his little mafia girlfriend planned the entire thing."

"But you and I both know that's not true."

"Do we?" Chief Pitman shook his head. "I don't know any such thing."

"There's something I probably should have told you this morning."

"Hm?" He narrowed his eyes. "Are you keeping things from me again, Blu?"

"Not intentionally. It may seem that way, but honestly, I didn't think it was important at the time."

"What is it, Blu?" He took a step closer to her. "Out with it."

"I might have seen someone climb out of the window of Hilda's house after I followed Oliver home."

"That's why it took you so long to get back to the house?" He shook his head. "I knew I should have had surveillance on you the whole time. Just like this morning. You think you can put yourself in danger without consequence. What if Oliver had seen you? What if he was armed?"

"Look, I realize now it might not have been the best choice, but it didn't seem like a bad idea at the time. Anyway, I saw this man climb out of Hilda's bedroom window."

"And that wasn't important?"

"After I found out about Marta, I didn't think so. I

figured that outing an affair between Hilda and some random person would only further hurt Oliver and do nothing to help the case."

"Oh, is that the problem? Did you get yourself a little crush on this Oliver?"

"No." Blu narrowed her eyes. "Not at all, thank you very much."

"Then why do you care so much if he gets hurt?"

"I don't think anyone should ever lose their whole family. His father is dead, his girlfriend is in jail for killing his father, and now he's going to find out his mother is having an affair?"

"That is rough." Chief Pitman nodded. "So, why are you telling me now?"

"I'm telling you because I saw Hilda and a man—who I believe to be the same man—at the skating rink this afternoon. AJ said that his name is Jack and he works at the shop that Hilda owns. If you ruled out Hilda as a suspect because he claimed to be at the shop with her, then I thought it could be possible that his claim was false."

"Wow." Chief Pitman frowned. "That does change things. I will have to go back and look that information over—which I probably would have done first thing this morning if you'd told me then."

"I'm sorry." Blu sighed. "Maybe I'm not so good at this crime-solving thing."

"Hey, don't say that." He smiled a little. "You have

brought me a lot of good information. You just have to give me the benefit of the doubt that I really am a human being. I have a heart too, Blu. I don't want to destroy lives. I want to solve crimes and I want to make sure that the guilty are prosecuted."

"At least we have that in common." Blu smiled a little. "I will try to be more forthcoming."

"In the spirit of that, I have some interesting information as well. Information that changes the entire dynamic of this case."

"What's that?"

"The medical examiner found something of interest in Emile's inside jacket pocket. I guess that it was overlooked the first time they went through his clothes."

"What was it?"

"A letter from someone. It threatened a lawsuit against his business. The language was quite harsh."

"Do you think that had something to do with why he was on the top of the lighthouse?"

"I think Emile was in over his head in more than one way. To be honest with you, if it wasn't for the medical examiner ruling this a murder I would be tempted to believe that Emile killed himself. He faced financial ruin and apparently his wife was having an affair. He had a lot to be upset about and not much to be happy about."

"But it's impossible that he killed himself?"

"It seems that way. The letter also doesn't change the fact that Marta was there at the time of the murder."

"Can you trace the letter to the person who wrote it?"

"We're working on it, but it was typed and it wasn't signed. So there's not much chance that we will be able to pin it down."

"Have you talked to Hilda about it?"

"Not yet. Now that I know about Jack, I can use that information and this letter to pressure her a bit. I'd like to see if I can rattle her. I don't like it when someone lies to me. It's clear that Hilda was hiding her relationship with Jack from me."

Blu tilted her head back and forth. "True, but that might be because she was ashamed, or she didn't want Oliver to find out."

"I guess when I speak to her we might be able to find some more information. From now on, you need to let me know everything that you find out. Understand?"

"Yes. There's something else."

"What?"

"Oliver knows that I'm the one who gave the information to create the sketch of Marta. I don't think he's telling the truth about knowing that Marta was there."

"Well, Marta hasn't spoken a word. She refuses to say anything to anyone, no matter how much we pressure her. She hasn't even asked for a phone call."

"That's interesting, don't you think?" Blu frowned.

"What do you mean?"

"Well, if her family is as connected as they seem,

don't you think she would be turning to them for help?"

"It's possible. Or they might have trained her never to speak to a cop, no matter what."

"True." Blu nodded. "You'll let me know how the interrogation goes?"

"Yes, I'll update you."

"Thanks." Blu smiled. "A team?"

"A team." He held his hand out to her.

Blu took it in a firm handshake. When she released it she was reminded of the way Oliver's hand shook when she'd handed him the beer. It struck her that he might not be afraid of being arrested, he might have been afraid that he was the next to die. If he knew about the letter that his father had received, maybe he thought that he was in danger too.

Blu sighed as she realized that sorting through all of the lies was going to be a larger task than finding actual evidence.

CHAPTER 21

As Blu walked back to her car, her mind returned to Marta. If Oliver really didn't know that she'd been at the lighthouse, could she have been the one that Emile was meeting with? Blu's stomach churned at the thought.

She sat in her car in the parking lot. She knew that she should head back to Maddie's and pick up the kids, but she also knew that they were safe and happy with her friend. After her conversation with Chief Pitman, she was even more confused. With Hilda and Jack added to the suspect list, Marta still couldn't be eliminated as the main suspect. If Marta wouldn't speak up to defend herself and Oliver wouldn't stop lying, then it was up to Blu to find out the truth about both of them.

So far she knew a good amount about Oliver's family. She needed to dig up more information about Marta.

She pulled out her phone and called Maddie.

"Hi, Blu. Everything okay?"

"Yes, but I have a question for you. You said you found some information about Marta on the Internet.

Would you be able to find out who she spent time with? Maybe a childhood friend or a family member?"

"Hang on, I can get that right now." She heard some keyboard strokes in the background. "Okay, are you there?"

"Yes, I'm here. Did you find something that fast?"

"Social media makes it pretty easy to find out who is important to people. Marta makes it even easier because there are so few people. First, of course, there's Oliver, then she mentions a cousin named Juan."

"Is there any information you can get me on Juan?"

"How about his place of employment?"

"That would be great."

"Mitch's Motors. I'll text you the address."

"Maddie, you're amazing."

"Keep that in mind, because all of this free babysitting is going to get paid back when Brennan gets together with his role-playing card game group."

"Oh, wow."

"What was that?"

"I mean, yes, of course. Thank you, Maddie."

"That's better." Maddie hung up the phone.

A moment later Blu received a text from her. She typed the address into her GPS and began driving. With the police station in her rearview mirror it occurred to her that she should let Chief Pitman know what she was doing. She bit her lip as she thought about it. She only intended to have a quick conversation with the guy.

When she drove up to the mechanic's shop, there was only one car in the parking lot. The white lettering on the glass indicated that the shop would close within the hour.

Blu tugged open the door and stepped inside. There were a few chairs grouped around a small table as well as a counter that wrapped around what looked like a storage area. She walked up to the counter and rang a small bell.

"We're closing." The man that walked up to the counter was tall and rail thin. He peered at her through thick glasses. "I can make you an appointment for tomorrow."

"Oh, no thank you. I'm only here to speak to one of your employees."

"Oh?" He raised an eyebrow. "You a cop or an angry girlfriend?"

"Neither." Blu smiled. "Just an old friend."

"Sure. Who are you looking for?"

"Juan."

"Oh." He nodded. "He's in the garage. But we're closing up soon. You can go around." He pointed to the side door.

"Thanks. And you are?

"Mitch." He pointed to the sign.

"Oh, of course." Blu smiled. "Thanks for your help, Mitch."

"Just don't make me regret it. I don't want any fights going on here."

"I promise. No drama." Blu hoped that it would be

the case.

She walked out through the side door and around toward the garage. The clink of metal against metal drew her attention. She poked her head around the corner of the open garage door. Although she didn't see anyone, she followed the sound.

She paused behind a jacked-up car. "Hello?"

"We're closed." The voice drifted out from under the car.

"Please, I just need a minute of your time."

She heard a labored sigh. A moment later a man rolled out from under the car.

He looked up at her. "What is it?"

Blu noticed his large size. His arms and chest were thicker than any man's she'd ever seen before. "Do you know Marta?"

"My cousin?" He ruffled a hand back through his sweaty hair. "Yeah, I know her."

"I'd just like to know what you think of her."

"That's what you interrupted me for? Are you aware that some people have to work for a living?"

"I work."

"Oh, yeah? What do you do?" He got to his feet and pulled a towel from his pocket. He stared at her as he rubbed some of the grease from his hands.

"I'm a nanny." Blu struggled to sound tough in the same moment that she admitted her profession.

"Huh?" He glanced around. "Where are the kids?"

Blu blinked. "Well, I'm not working right at this moment. Well, actually I am, but they're with a friend."

"A friend?" He chuckled and shoved the towel back into his pocket. "Doesn't sound like working to me."

"Listen, I was just hoping that you could give me an idea of what Marta is like. Was she involved in your family's business?"

He squinted at her. "You mean the shop?"

"No, that's not what I mean. The other business."

He chuckled. "Well, you're one brave nanny, aren't you?" He shook his head. "What do you know about the family business?"

"I know that it might be the reason a good man ended up dead."

He narrowed his eyes. "Marta had nothing to do with that. It's ridiculous that they arrested her. She had nothing to do with anything the family is involved in."

"And you?" Blu folded her arms across her chest.

"And me?" He smirked. "What's wrong? Can't you make a snap judgment from my muscles and my tattoos?"

"I'm asking." Blu kept her feet planted on the ground despite the fact that her instincts pleaded with her to run.

"Okay. Well, I used to be. Alright? I'm not going to admit to anything in particular, but yes, I used to be involved."

"What happened to change your mind?"

"Marta happened. When she was born—you know, she was just this cute little baby. No one thought twice about her. But from the moment she could talk, I knew she was going to change everything. She was bold, always telling people what they were doing wrong—that they should do better, be better. But not in a mean way—like she believed in them. She believed in me for some strange reason." He laughed. "It was crazy, but that kid got under my skin. She got me to go straight. Now, look what she gets for it. She's locked away because of her last name."

"She was at the scene of a murder."

"If she was there, it wasn't to kill anyone. If she was there, it was to protect someone." He held her gaze. "Make no mistake, Marta isn't the villain. She's the hero. No one will ever be able to tell me different."

"Maybe she gave in to the pressure of her family? Maybe she realized she couldn't escape her last name?"

CHAPTER 22

Juan drew a deep breath, then blew it back out slowly. "Marta was in love. Okay? She wouldn't do anything to ruin that. Here's the thing that is going to make it even harder for her to look innocent. Emile, Oliver's father, was a real jerk."

"What?" Blu raised an eyebrow. "How so?"

"He was always trying to break Marta and Oliver up. In fact, he even threatened to cut Oliver out of his will if he continued to date her. Poor Oliver would never have his chance to run the hot dog cart." He rolled his eyes. "But Oliver didn't care."

"Wait, why would Emile have a problem with Marta?"

"Because of her family. He was afraid that Marta was involved—that she'd pull Oliver into it, I guess. He didn't even give her a chance. Marta was sure that Oliver would leave her, but he didn't."

"Did Oliver ever make any threats against his father? Was he angry at him?"

"Oliver?" Juan raised an eyebrow. "I don't think that kid has ever said a disrespectful word. He wasn't angry at his father. He wished that he would accept Marta, but he wasn't angry at him."

"Are you sure about that?"

"Sure I'm sure. I wouldn't have let Marta be with any hothead. There's been enough pain in our family. She's too good for that."

"So you're quite protective of her?"

"Yes, I am. She's been the only bright light in my life."

"It must have really bothered you that Emile treated her so harshly then." Blu met his eyes. "Marta is innocent and Emile treated her like a common criminal."

"Now you're putting words into my mouth," said Juan.

"Am I wrong?" Blu watched him. "I mean, Marta might as well have been scum on Emile's shoe. He didn't think she was good enough for his son. Marta was nothing but trash to him. And maybe he was right. Maybe she saw her chance to get rid of an obstacle in her life and she decided to take it. Maybe murder runs in her blood."

"You shut your mouth!" Juan lunged forward so fast that Blu had to jump back to avoid him. "You have no idea what you're talking about. Marta is a good person! She would never hurt anyone."

Pinned between Juan's angry stare and the concrete wall of the garage, Blu had nowhere to go. Despite her fear, she still wanted the truth.

"Not like you, right, Juan?" She glared into his eyes. "Not like her big cousin who would do anything to protect her. Maybe she cried to you one too many times about the way that Emile treated her. Maybe you decided to pay her back for being the light of your life the only way that you knew how."

"You're wrong." He didn't move an inch away from her. "You're wrong about everything."

"I don't think I am, Juan." Blu searched his eyes. "I think Marta may be innocent, but I think you couldn't hold back. Emile is dead because he hurt the best thing in your life. Isn't that right?"

"Is there a problem here?" Mitch stood at the entrance of the garage. When he saw Blu pinned against the wall he rushed forward. "Back off, Juan!" He grabbed the large man's shoulder. "Do you want to end up behind bars again?"

Juan snarled at Blu and pulled away from Mitch's touch. "She's telling lies, Mitch. That's all it is."

"I gave you a chance to straighten out your life, Juan. Don't make me wish I hadn't. Get out of here!"

"But I'm not finished—"

"—Oh, you're finished!" Mitch scowled.

Despite the fact that Mitch was frail in comparison, Juan lowered his head. He turned and walked out of the garage without another word.

"I'm sorry, miss. He's really not a bad guy. I don't

know what got into him."

"It's alright." Blu narrowed her eyes. "Did you say behind bars again?"

"Yes. Juan has a few arrests under his belt, but he grew up in a rough area. So did I. I try to give the guys who want to change their lives a chance."

"Was he here with you two days ago?"

"No. We were closed." He frowned. "What has he gotten himself into now?"

"Has he been acting strange at all? Maybe making more phone calls than usual?"

"No, nothing. He's a hard worker—always early and never a problem." He paused for a moment, then winced.

"What is it?" Blu studied him. She had a feeling that Mitch was much more comfortable talking to her than he would be to any police officer.

"There was one strange thing. I caught him in my office last week. None of my guys are allowed in my office. It's where I keep the petty cash and customer's information. It's just a precaution I take because you never know who you can trust."

"I understand." Blu nodded. "What was he doing?"

"I thought at first that he was stealing from me, and I told him that. I threatened to fire him. But he was only printing something out. The cash drawer was locked. Nothing was missing."

"Did you see what he printed?"

"It was a letter. He said he was applying for some

kind of technical school. I thought it was a good thing, so I let it slide. But to be honest with you, it bothered me that he didn't just ask me instead of sneaking around."

"He doesn't have a computer at home?"

Mitch laughed and shook his head. "You haven't spent a lot of time poor, have you?"

Blu frowned. "I thought his family was pretty well off."

"His family, if you want to call them that, sure. All dirty money. But Juan left all of that. He was staying in a room barely bigger than my office. He didn't have anything, but he didn't care. Whatever you think he's involved in, I really hope that you're wrong. Juan might have a temper, but I've never doubted that he was trying to make a real change."

"What about his cousin Marta? Have you ever seen her around here?"

"Oh, the young girl?" He nodded. "Sure. Before I let him rebuild one of our junkers she would drop him off and pick him up every day. A real sweetheart. She would bring us all lunch sometimes."

"Thanks for your time." Blu smiled. "Sorry for the drama."

"Just keep in mind—I do think Juan's a good guy. I've never seen him act like this before."

"I will."

As Blu walked out of the garage she noticed a large trashcan by the door. Inside the trashcan was a wrapper from Emile's hot dog cart. Her heart sank when she saw it. Sometimes she hated to be right.

If Juan had been at the lighthouse to protect Marta, the only question was, did Marta know about it? Did Oliver?

CHAPTER 23

When Blue arrived at Maddie's house her heart still raced. The memory of how angry Juan had become when she'd baited him had left her feeling very unsettled.

She greeted the kids with a wide smile. "Did you guys have fun today?"

"Yes." Marley giggled. "Joey has a girlfriend."

"What?" Blu's eyes widened.

She looked at Maddie, who grinned.

"Relax, his girlfriend is one of Brennan's friends. I don't think they have much of a future, but don't tell Joey that."

"Isn't he too young for that?" Blu sank down on the couch beside Maddie.

"Not according to him. I think he's just trying to be like Brennan."

"He really loves spending time with him. Thank you for helping me out so much, Maddie."

"Did anything come of it?"

"I think I may have figured out who the guilty person

is, but I think it's only going to make things more complicated. Anyway, I'd better get going with the kids before Rachel gets home. Tonight is family dinner."

"Good luck."

"Thanks." Blu smiled.

"In case you were wondering, AJ stayed with us until we came back to the house. He's really one of those rare nice guys."

"He seems to be." Blu stood up.

"Are you really going to let this pass you by, Blu?" Maddie looked up at her.

"He is amazing, Maddie. But we're also two very different people, and our lives are taking us in different directions. What's the point of setting myself up for heartbreak?"

"Hm. Maybe it doesn't have to be that way."

Blu smiled and leaned down to give Maddie a hug. She loved her friend, but Maddie was more of a dreamer than she would ever be.

When they arrived at the beach house Blu started to prepare dinner. She placed a call to Chief Pitman to update him about her encounter with Juan.

When he answered, his voice was strained. "I'm sorry I haven't called you about the interrogation, Blu, but there's really nothing to report. She's still refusing to talk."

"Well I found out some interesting things about her cousin Juan today."

"Who?"

"I might have pinpointed him as an important person in her life."

"And?"

"I went to speak with him."

"Blu."

"I know, I know, but just listen. While I was there I saw his temper, and I also spoke to his boss. It's clear to me that Juan is very protective of Marta, and his boss said that he printed out a letter last week. You might want to go yourself to speak with them both."

"I'll do that."

"I'll send you the address. I wasn't going behind your back, I just didn't want you to waste resources if it turned out to be nothing."

"It doesn't sound like nothing."

"No it doesn't. I also saw a wrapper from Emile's hot dog cart in the trashcan at the garage. I think Juan lost his temper and decided to get rid of Emile in an attempt to protect his cousin."

"What about the letter? You think it was just a ploy?"

"Sure. Maybe Juan sent it to him, asked him to meet with him at the top of the lighthouse so that he could kill him."

"And Marta was there because?"

"That part I haven't been able to figure out."

"It's a lot of guessing."

"But Chief Pitman, the one thing that has remained

consistent through all of this is that everyone I speak to tells me how wonderful Marta is. There's no evidence that she's ever been involved in any crime. I'm sure of it. Marta didn't do this. Her cousin might have. But she didn't do it."

"Blu, unless you can give me some solid evidence that clears her or implicates someone else, there's nothing I can do here. Marta won't even speak to defend herself. With her family's history and her presence there, as well as her relationship with Oliver, she is a great suspect." He sighed. "And I'm not convinced that she and Oliver didn't cook this up."

"Juan told me that Emile didn't want Oliver to date Marta. Oliver, who in every other way has been a good son, has never been in any kind of trouble, defied his father and continued to date her."

"Okay, but Blu, that's not unusual. Oliver is young, He thinks he's in love. Everything is so much more intense and dramatic at that age. That only puts him at a higher risk of doing something foolish like murdering his father. You can't really expect me to think that true love is a reason not to pursue a suspect."

Blu shook her head. "That's not what I expect at all. But you're missing one very important point."

"What's that?"

"Hilda knew about Marta. We know why Oliver would lie to protect Marta. He loves her. But Hilda, who supported their relationship, didn't even mention that

Oliver had a girlfriend. She claimed she didn't recognize the sketch. With so much drama in the family around Marta, how could that be a mistake? She omitted the information on purpose. Why?"

Chief Pitman was quiet for several seconds until he spoke again slowly. "Because she knew that Marta didn't kill her husband."

"Exactly. If Hilda was really a grieving widow, if someone told her that her son's girlfriend was at the scene of the murder, why would she pretend not to know her? There's only one reason. Either she knew that Marta did it because she asked Marta to do it, or she knew that Marta didn't do it, because she knows who really did."

"The question is, who is Hilda trying to protect?"

"Her son is the obvious choice. But perhaps it is her boyfriend? We know that Oliver wasn't on the top of the lighthouse when Emile was thrown over. Even if he was involved somehow, he is not the killer."

"Even when we figure out for sure who the killer is, we're not going to have the whole picture. Whoever did this, likely did not act alone."

"But like I said, Juan printed out the letter."

"He printed out a letter. We don't know if it was the same letter."

"There's only one person that knows the whole truth of what happened on the top of that lighthouse."

"Marta." Chief Pitman cleared his throat. "And she's not talking."

"What would you say to letting me in on your next interrogation?"

"I'd say it's unconventional."

"I was able to bait Juan into showing me his temper; I might be able to do the same with Marta."

"It's worth a shot. I'm certainly not getting anything out of her. Can you meet me in the morning at the station?"

Blu set the last plate down on the table. She looked at Marley and Joey in the living room. She couldn't ask Maddie to watch the kids again.

"I'm not sure if I can get away."

"I'll tell you what, bring the kids in with you. I'm sure we can find a way to occupy them."

"Okay." Blu brightened. "They would love that."

She hung up the phone just as Rachel walked in the door.

"Hi, everybody!" She smiled as the kids ran up to hug her.

Blu was touched by the joy that consumed Rachel's features. As much as she enjoyed her time with the kids, she knew it wasn't the same feeling as a mother had with her children.

Maddie's words played back through her mind.

Are you really going to let that pass you by? Maybe AJ was her only chance at the kind of love that would lead to marriage and a family for herself one day.

CHAPTER 24

Early the next morning Blu got the kids dressed and fed.

"We have somewhere special to go this morning."

"Where?" Joey shoved his foot into his shoe.

"The police station."

"Oh, yay!" Marley smiled. "I like the badges."

"Why are we going to the police station?" Joey looked at Blu. "Are you in trouble or something?"

"No, no one's in trouble. Chief Pitman said he'd have something for the two of you to do today. So we're going to go and see what it is."

"I hope it's handcuffs!" Marley jumped up and down.

"What?" Blu laughed.

"I'm going to lock Joey up!"

"No, you're not!" Joey stuck out his tongue at her. "You're the one that needs to go to annoying little sister jail."

"Alright, alright, let's be nice." She gave Joey a look. "No one is going to be cuffed, and no one is going to jail.

Let's go see what Chief Pitman has set up for you."

She led them out to the car with the hope that Chief Pitman had come up with something. When they arrived at the police station Chief Pitman greeted them in the lobby.

"There are my junior detectives!" He smiled at the kids. "I have a case I need your help with. Officer Tinsley is going to help you. Okay?"

"A case? Like a real crime?" Joey's eyes widened. "What is it?"

"It's the case of a missing cat. Mr. Hooper's cat disappeared and we need to figure out where it went. Do you two think you could help with that?"

"Oh yes!" Marley clapped her hands. "We'll find the kitty."

"Great. Officer Tinsley, your cat detectives are here."

"Wonderful!" The young officer grinned at them. "Who's ready to go for a ride?"

"We are!" Joey grinned. "Wait. Do I get handcuffs?"

Officer Tinsley looked up at Blu. Blu shook her head firmly.

"Not this time." Officer Tinsley smiled. "But I'll let you use the siren."

"Cool!"

As Officer Tinsley led the two kids away, Blu shook her head. "Wow, I can't believe you thought of that. What a great adventure for them."

"Actually it was AJ's idea."

"Oh?"

"I called him last night to see if he could come up with anything. He said the kids have probably been around you enough to be detectives themselves."

Blu smiled. "I'll have to thank him."

"You should." Chief Pitman held her gaze for a moment. "He seems a bit smitten with you."

Blu stared back at him. She wasn't sure what to say. "He's been very kind to me."

"Hm." Chief Pitman tilted his head toward one of the closed doors along the hallway. "I've already got her in the interrogation room. Are you sure you're up for this?"

"Yes. I've been thinking about it all morning. I think if she knows that Juan is in trouble, she's going to come clean."

"Or lie through her teeth to protect her cousin."

"Either way she'll be talking."

"True."

Chief Pitman led her to the door and opened it up. Marta looked tiny behind the large wooden table. She didn't even look in their direction as the two stepped inside. It was easy to see that the repeated interrogations were taking a toll. Her eyelids drooped and her lips were chapped.

"Hi, Marta." Blu sat down beside her. "I'm here to talk to you about what happened."

Marta rolled her eyes and looked away from her.

"This is all I've been getting." Chief Pitman shook his

head.

"Marta, I don't believe that you killed Emile."

"Blu." Chief Pitman stepped up beside her.

"It's okay, Chief. It's time that someone is honest with her." Blu looked back at Marta. "I don't believe that you're guilty, Marta, but that doesn't matter. You look very guilty. That's really all that matters. So you're going to go to prison for a very long time." Blu tried to meet her eyes. "That is just how it is."

Marta shrugged and stared hard at the table. "Marta, you're either going to talk, or you're going to spend the rest of your life in jail. What do you think Oliver will do without you?"

Marta narrowed her eyes. Her lips tensed, as did the rest of her body.

Blu continued. "Yes. He'll be all alone—his father dead, his mother cheating, the love of his life behind bars. Oliver is a strong young man, but do you think he can really survive all that? You're the only good thing in his life, Marta. Are you really going to take that away from him?"

Marta blinked a few times before Blu noticed the glimmer of tears in her eyes.

"Marta!" Chief Pitman slammed his hand down on the table in front of her.

Marta jumped in her chair.

"I'm not in the business of putting away innocent people. If you didn't do this, then speak up for yourself, girl. You have your entire future ahead of you. What happened on the top of that lighthouse?"

Marta cleared her throat. "I can't say."

CHAPTER 25

"Yes, you can." Blu leaned across the table. She looked into Marta's tear-filled eyes. "Is it your family you're protecting? Is it Juan?"

"Juan?" Marta's eyes widened. "Why are you asking about Juan?"

"He's a big man. He could have easily thrown Emile over the side of the lighthouse. Was he there with you that day? Is that what happened?"

"No!" Marta looked from one face then to the other. "You have to leave Juan alone. He had nothing to do with any of this."

"I don't believe that, Marta." Blu stood up and leaned over the back of Marta's chair. "I believe that Juan did something misguided to protect you, and now you think that by keeping your mouth shut about what happened, you're protecting him. But you're not. Nothing you're doing right now is going to protect Juan. The truth is that Emile didn't deserve to die. He was a good father and a good husband who was only doing what he thought was best for his son. No one deserves to die for that. But Juan decided to take matters into his own hands. He hated the way that Emile treated you. He hated that you weren't good enough for Emile, and he wanted to make Emile suffer because of that. Didn't he?"

Blu placed a hand on the curve of Marta's shoulder. She could feel the young woman trembling. "He did what you weren't brave enough to do."

"No." Marta breathed the word out. "No you're wrong. That's not what happened at all."

"Then tell us what happened." Chief Pitman rested both hands on the table and stared hard into Marta's eyes. "You're the only one that knows the truth, Marta. You have all the power. If you speak, everything changes. If you don't, you go right back in your cell, and I promise you that I will find a way to put Juan in the one right next to you."

"No!" Marta gasped. "He's just getting back on his feet. None of this was his fault. If I had just walked away from Oliver, none of this would have happened. It's my fault. It doesn't matter if I wasn't the one who pushed him over. I was the one who caused it, so I should be the one to pay the price."

"Marta, that's not how it works." Blu sat down beside her again. She placed her hand over Marta's. "You may love Juan, but he's the one that killed Emile."

"No, he's not." Marta blinked back tears. "He didn't do it. I saw who did it. It wasn't him."

Blu and Chief Pitman exchanged looks.

"What about the letter, Marta? Did you know about that?" Blu asked.

Marta closed her eyes.

"It was stupid. It was so stupid. I'm sorry." Her cheeks reddened as tears coasted down along them. "I never meant for any of this to happen."

"Did you know about the letter?"

Marta was silent for a long moment as her body shook with the force of her tears. Then she drew a deep breath.

"I don't want to say anything else. I'm not saying another word. If you want to know who killed Emile so bad, you figure it out." She folded her arms on the table and rested her head on them.

Blu and Chief Pitman exchanged a look across the top of her head. Blu knew that Marta was not going to say another word.

"Marta, I wish that I could help you. You're making a mistake." Blu shook her head.

"The only mistake I ever made was believing that love would be enough. I knew that I should stay away from Oliver, but I just couldn't." She gulped out her words. "I couldn't. He wouldn't let me."

"Did Oliver force you to do something?" Blu leaned closer to her.

"Yes!" Marta looked up into Blu's eyes.

"What was it, Marta? What did he force you to do?"

"He forced me to believe in myself, and that I was

worthy of his love. He forced me to think that somehow we could be together. He was wrong, I was wrong, and now Emile is dead." She wiped at her eyes. "The worst part is that Emile was right. He was right to tell Oliver to stay away from me. I caused nothing but pain."

As the tears flowed down the young woman's cheeks, something within Blu awakened. Perhaps it was a maternal need, or a deep sense of sisterhood; whatever it was, she put her arms around Marta and held her.

"Blu you can't do that." Chief Pitman moved to stop her, but Blu shook her head.

She held Marta close in her arms and let the woman cry against her shoulder.

In that moment she knew that she'd never be able to walk away from the case—not until the truth came out.

CHAPTER 26

Outside of the interrogation room Chief Pitman paced back and forth. "You shouldn't have done that."

"I had to do that."

"She's a prisoner."

"She's a person." Blu shook her head. "You can't forget that. At least I can't. Can't you see how much she is hurting?"

"Blu, she could be involved in a murder and is refusing to give us any good information to work with. Am I really supposed to feel sympathy for that?"

Blu sighed. "I don't know what you're supposed to feel. But I do know that Marta has never had anyone except for Oliver. Whatever she's carrying on her shoulders is much heavier than any burden I've ever had to carry."

Chief Pitman paused in front of her. "You have a good heart, Blu. But there's no room for that in police work. The fact is that if she doesn't give us something, we're stuck. She's going to be the one that pays the price.

She'll have to take her chances with a jury and hope that it's filled with people like you."

"I think we can do better than that."

"What's your plan?" Chief Pitman studied her.

"I'm not sure yet, but I know I have to do something. Maybe we're looking at this from the wrong angle."

"I'm not sure how else to look at it."

"We keep thinking about who killed Emile, but I think the better question is why did he have to die? Was it because he stood in the way of Oliver and Marta's relationship? Did he borrow money from the wrong person? What was it that he did that was so terrible it warranted him being thrown to his death?"

"Love, money, revenge—those are the three most common reasons for murder, Blu."

"Well, then that's where I'll start. I'll let you know what I find out."

"Alright." He nodded. "In the meantime, I'm going to pick up Juan. I want to see what he has to say about all this."

"Keep me up-to-date."

"I will."

As Chief Pitman walked away, Blu spotted Joey and Marley with officer Tinsley. Joey had a bandage on the back of his right hand.

"What happened?" Blu looked at the bandage.

"I found the cat." Joey smiled proudly.

"I'm sorry, ma'am, he got to the cat before I could."

Blu smiled as she met Joey's eyes. "I guess you are a great cat detective."

"I try." Joey giggled.

"That was one mean cat." Marley shivered. "I think I want a bunny."

"Well, we might have to wait until we get back to the city for that." Blu grinned. "For now, why don't we go have some lunch at home?"

"Can we invite AJ?"

Blu thought about the question for a moment.

"Not today, sweetie. Today I think it should be just us. We can have lunch outside on the patio and then play in the sand. Okay?"

"Okay." Marley smiled.

Blu drove the kids back to the beach house. She prepared a picnic-style lunch to take outside. As she settled the kids at the patio table she thought about the three motivations that the murderer might have had.

Emile was a stern man, who clearly had certain standards for his family. Hilda implied that he was cheating on her, but so far neither she nor Chief Pitman had turned up any evidence of that. If he had a mistress, where was she? If he didn't, then why would Hilda believe that he did?

The kids chatted about their adventure with Officer Tinsley as Blu thought through all of the possibilities. She felt as if she just couldn't make the connection. Hilda certainly was lying about a lot of things.

Just when Blu was about to set the kids loose in the sand, Rachel walked out through the back door.

"Hi, guys!" She smiled. "Guess what? My meeting was canceled. So I get to spend the afternoon with you."

The kids cheered.

"Look, Mom, I got sliced by a cat!" Joey lifted his hand and pointed to the bandage.

"Oh, wow. I bet there's a story there." Rachel laughed.

"Rachel, let me make you some lunch."

"No, it's fine. I already ate. If you wouldn't mind running to the shop and picking up some milk, I'd really appreciate it. I meant to stop on my way home and forgot."

"Of course, no problem at all."

"Just bring it home with you when you can. You're welcome to have the afternoon off. Alright?"

"Are you sure?"

"Yes, I could use some playtime and some beach time."

"I'll be back in time to get dinner ready."

"That would be perfect."

"Bye, guys!" Blu waved to the children.

Each one grabbed one of Rachel's hands and tugged her out onto the sand. Blu smiled as she watched. She was glad that they were all getting some playtime, but she was also glad that she would have the chance to do some more investigating.

As soon as she grabbed her keys she knew where she was headed. She could pick up some milk after hunting around for a little more evidence.

CHAPTER 27

Blu pulled the car to a stop a few blocks down from Hilda's shop. She didn't want to give Hilda any warning that she was there. As she approached the shop, she noticed that the windows were dark. It struck her that, with a death in the family, they might have closed up for a few days.

When she tried the door it didn't budge. Still, she lingered outside the shop. She was sure that the proof she needed was inside.

She started to turn away when she heard a voice coming from inside.

"I'm so glad it's over."

Blu recognized the voice as Hilda's.

"It's so amazing to finally be free. I never thought it would happen. I really didn't. I thought I was going to be stuck with him for the rest of my life. All of his nitpicking and tradition. He smelled like a hot dog, even right out of the shower. Disgusting."

Blu's eyes widened as she listened to the hateful words. She knew that Hilda wasn't fond of her husband, but the fact that she was happy about his death was a different matter.

Hilda paused as if she might have been on the phone with someone, then continued. "I feel a little bad for Oliver. He's pretty torn up over it. But he'll move on and see it was for the best. His father would have messed up his life, just like he ruined mine. Marta will get out when they can't find any physical evidence. She never should have been there in the first place." She clucked her tongue.

Blu's heart skipped a beat. She pulled out her phone and sent Chief Pitman a text.

Meet me at Hilda's shop. She's definitely involved.

Then she pressed her ear against the door to hear more.

If Hilda was still on the phone, she was too far away for Blu to hear her. Minutes passed. Blu didn't want to leave and give Hilda the chance to escape. She wanted to confront the woman face-to-face.

Out of respect, she waited for Chief Pitman to text, call, or show up, but time was quickly passing. She checked the time on her phone again. There were still no texts or calls from Chief Pitman.

Blu's impatience increased with every minute that passed. She tried to resist the urge to take matters into her own hands. When she checked her phone again she began to feel irritated. Wasn't the case important enough to Chief Pitman that he'd make it a priority to get there? She shoved her phone deep into her pocket and crossed her arms.

There was a crash inside the store.

Her heart lurched. Something bad had happened inside. She was sure of it. Was it Hilda? Was it Jack? Or could it be both?

A horrible thought crossed her mind. What if Jack was killing Hilda? Or even vice versa?

She stared in through the window, but the store was too dark for her to see inside. Could she really stand outside while another murder was potentially being committed?

She started to reach for her phone to check it again, but decided against it. Instead, she walked around the side of the shop and then behind it. She saw Hilda's car parked there but no other cars.

When Blu tried the back door it swung open. As quietly as she could. she slipped inside.

On the floor was a large amount of cans and boxes. It looked like an entire shelf had been tipped over. Blu picked her way through it to the other side.

Just when she was going to call out to see if Hilda was there a large shadow filled the doorway. Blu took in a sharp breath as the shadow moved toward her. Within a few steps she was able to tell that it was Jack, Hilda's boyfriend.

"Jack, what are you doing here?"

"I work here."

'The shop is closed."

"Then I guess I should be asking you what you're doing here." He crossed his arms.

Blu looked past him toward the main part of the store. "Where's Hilda?"

"She's not here. Why?"

"I know she's here. I heard her from outside the shop."

"Is that so?" He shrugged. "Then I guess you just missed her."

"Did you hurt her, Jack?"

Jack took two large steps and within seconds was nearly on top of Blu. "Why would you ask me that? I love Hilda."

"What did you do with her, Jack? I know she was here."

"She left, alright. When I got here, she hung out with me and then went out the back. On her way out she knocked over the rack." He tilted his head toward the mess on the floor. "I was just coming back here to clean it up. I think the real question, is, what are you doing in here?"

"I came in to check on Hilda. When I heard the crash, I thought maybe she was hurt."

"Oh?" He leaned a bit closer to her. "Just what else did you hear?"

Blu only stared back at him in response. "Too much."

He narrowed his eyes. "I guess that means I'll have to

deal with you."

Blu took a step back and stared at the man before her. "You don't have to do this."

"That's where you're wrong. I wouldn't have had to do anything else if you had just stayed out of things. Now I have no choice."

"How can you just kill people? It's a horrible thing to take another life."

"You're right, it is." He frowned. "But it's worth it to me. If it means I get to be with Hilda, it's worth it."

"I think you should think this through, Jack. What if Hilda decides that she isn't really in love with you? What if you're the one who has to spend the rest of your life in prison? Is that something that you really want to risk?"

"I'll be fine. I would go to prison a thousand times to protect Hilda."

"Jack, she's using you. She is never going to marry you. She has her son to think about."

"With Emile gone Oliver will learn to accept me. Sure, it will take some time, but he'll eventually come to know me as a father figure."

CHAPTER 28

Blu stared at Jack as her heart raced. It was clear to her that he was not in his right mind. His loyalty to Hilda bordered on obsession.

"What is Oliver going to think when he finds out that you were the one who killed his father?"

"That was an accident." Jack gritted his teeth. "It was never supposed to happen like that."

"What was supposed to happen, Jack?" Blu inched her way back toward the door of the shop. She continued to stall him. "What did the two of you plan?"

"We were just going to scare him. That was all. Hilda thought that if we scared him enough, he'd give up and run. We sent the letter saying that he was going to be sued. Then I went to meet with him—just for the purpose of scaring him. I was only going to threaten him, make him realize it would be best for him to just take off. Then he'd be out of our lives forever."

"But that didn't happen." Blu narrowed her eyes. "Why didn't it happen that way?"

"Because of that stupid girl. I was scaring him. I had

him pushed back over the railing, just to give him a taste of what it would be like. Then this girl pops up out of the blue. She started to shout at me. She interrupted everything. While she distracted me, Emile pulled off my mask. Then he said my name. That was it. He knew who I was. I couldn't risk Hilda going to jail."

"Or you, isn't that right, Jack? Was this really ever about Hilda or was it about protecting your own skin?"

"I got scared. I needed to go after the girl, and I needed to keep Emile quiet. So I shoved him a little too hard and over he went. I just didn't expect that to happen. I didn't."

Blu shook her head. "All you had to do was be honest. If you and Hilda told Emile the truth then maybe none of this would have happened."

"I know!" He sighed. "I begged Hilda to just let it be known that we were together. But she refused. She said that Emile was loyal to her, that he adored her, and he would never let her go."

"But she doesn't feel the same?"

"Hilda was forced to marry Emile. Her father was friends with Emile's father. He thought Emile would be a perfect match, and wouldn't leave Hilda alone until she agreed to marry him. She was barely nineteen. She was just a girl. She never had the chance to know what real love was. Is that a good man? A man who would marry because his parents told him to?"

"It's not for you to judge. If Hilda wanted to leave

she could have divorced her husband. Why did he have to die?"

Jack shook his head. "He never would have let her go. He was too traditional for that. Hilda got it in her head that we could find one of Marta's relatives to help us out. She asked Marta, but Marta got upset and told her she didn't want any part of it."

"So Hilda went to Juan herself."

"Yes. She told him that she wanted Emile gone. Juan was the one that came up with the idea of the lawsuit. He said it would be enough to scare Emile away. But it wasn't. Emile wanted a meeting to discuss the lawsuit. I was just going to scare him. But I guess Juan must have told Marta what we were planning. I don't know why she showed up there—I guess to protect Emile. Stupid girl."

"She wasn't stupid. She was brave. She knew that you were going to hurt Emile and she wanted to stop you. Now she's trying to protect her cousin, because he was involved with all of this."

"It doesn't matter now, does it?" He smirked. "We're all alone here, you and I."

"You're not going to hurt me, Jack." Blu watched him as he moved closer to her.

"What makes you think that?" He raised an eyebrow.

"I'm stronger than you think. Emile never had a chance, did he? You just shoved him over. You didn't give him a chance to fight back. But I'll fight back. You might be able to get rid of me, but I will leave my mark on you. I will make sure that there's plenty of evidence to prove who hurt me."

Blu was glad that the words coming out of her mouth didn't reflect the crazy nervous beating of her heart as she watched Jack in front of her.

"I got away with one murder, I don't think I'm going to have too much trouble with another one." He reached his hands out as if to grab her throat.

Blu swung her hands up to block him before he could grab her. His hands fell away but only for a split second. Then he surged at her again. She tried to duck out of the way but he was too fast. He pushed her back against the wall, then stepped in front of her to make sure that she had no way to escape.

"You can fight as much as you want, but no one is going to rescue you. Things went sideways with Emile, but this won't be any accident." He grabbed her by the throat again and began to squeeze.

Blu struggled to get free, but the more that she wriggled, the tighter his grip became. Her vision began to blur. Her chest ached for air. Her mind filled with all of the things that she'd never had the chance to do. Just when she thought she was about to lose consciousness, the side door was flung open.

"Get on your knees, Jack." Chief Pitman pointed his gun right at him.

Jack's eyes sparked with heat as he looked from Blu to the gun that was pointed at him. His grip loosened on

Blu's neck.

"Let her go, Jack. I have no problem doing what I have to do to protect her. Understand?"

Blu looked over at Chief Pitman as she drew a deep breath of air. "He's done something to Hilda!"

"Shut up!" Jack sank down to his knees. "Why can't you ever just keep your mouth shut?" He glared at Blu.

"Where's Hilda?" She glared back at him. "What did you do to her?"

"I told you, I didn't do anything! She left right before you came in."

CHAPTER 29

Chief Pitman rushed up to Jack and pinned his arms behind his back. Blu heard the click of the handcuffs and finally believed that she was safe. As she rubbed the curve of her neck she drew in another breath.

"I don't believe you!" Blu shouted at Jack. "Where's Hilda?"

"Just call her!"

"Quiet." Chief Pitman pulled him to his feet. "Blu, what happened here?"

"Jack killed Emile. Hilda was in on the plan."

"I did what I had to do. I did what she wanted me to do, whether she knew it or not. Hilda tried to tell me she just wanted to scare Emile, but I knew better. She wanted him gone. That's why she told Marta that Juan was part of it all. She knew that Marta would try to interfere."

"But she's not the one who pushed Emile, is she?" Blu crossed her arms and kept her distance from the two.

"I'm calling for backup. We'll find Hilda and get the whole story. Do you need an ambulance, Blu?"

"No. I think I'm fine." Blu frowned. She wasn't fine.

She was terrified. She could still feel Jack's hands around her neck.

"Let's go." Chief Pitman pulled Jack out of the shop. Blu followed at a safe distance.

"Blu? Are you okay?" AJ jogged up to her from the front of the shop.

"What are you doing here?"

"My uncle called me when he thought something might be wrong. I guess he was right." He watched as Chief Pitman pushed Jack toward the patrol car.

"What happened?"

"It's a long story." Blu shook her head, then rested it against AJ's shoulder.

"Are you sure that you're okay?"

"Yes. I just can't believe that it was Jack all along."

"He didn't act alone. I'm guessing Hilda had an influence on him."

"Oh, I'm certain of that. Jack claimed he did what he did out of love. Maybe Hilda thought she did it to protect her son. Through all of it, Emile was just a victim. He never even had the chance to defend himself." Blu sighed as she glanced over at Jack in the pack of the patrol car. "I'm just relieved that it's over—and that Marta and Oliver are innocent in all of it. At least they still have each other."

"That's true." AJ wrapped his arm around her and pulled her close. "I think it's sweet how they never doubted one another, not even once."

"That we know about. We only know what they were telling us."

"Always the cynic, hm?" He smiled.

"Maybe." She turned around to face him. "Not all the time. But today I think I've earned my right. I went into that shop because I thought Hilda needed my protection. Instead, I was the one that ended up being saved, thanks to your uncle. I'm starting to think that my instincts are rusty."

"Not at all. Your instinct was to help, and there's nothing rusty about that. Do you want me to drive you home?"

"Yes, please. I'm supposed to be making dinner. I need to pick up milk."

AJ smiled and looked into her eyes.

"Take a breath, Blu. I'll take care of it. Just come with me." He walked her over to his jeep.

When Blu climbed in, her heart finally began to slow. She closed her eyes as the engine roared to life. AJ's hand brushed over hers, then closed over her fingers. Blu pulled her hand away in a gentle motion.

"I'm sorry." AJ glanced over at her.

"It's okay, AJ. I'm just tired."

"It's more than that. Isn't it, Blu?" He frowned. "I know that this isn't the right time to ask you this, but I don't think I can hold it in any longer. You're never going to give me a chance, are you?"

Blu looked over at him, still dazed from her

encounter with Jack. "I'm sorry if it seems that way, but summer is almost over. Don't you think our chance has passed?"

"I don't think it will ever pass, Blu. It's not like the city is on another planet."

"It might as well be." Blu stared down at her hands. "Don't you think that our lives are too different, AJ?"

"No, I don't." He parked in the parking lot of a store. "I think that our lives are whatever we allow them to be. I think that sometimes life isn't about making the choice that makes the most sense. You trust your instincts all the time when you're trying to get to the truth. So, why can't you trust your instincts about me?" He stepped out of the jeep before she could answer.

Blu saw him disappear into the store. She remembered a time before college, a time when she believed that everything was spontaneous and life was filled with endless potential. She was a different person then. But AJ reminded her of who she once was. He spoke what he felt and he trusted his instincts.

When he returned to the jeep with the gallon of milk Blu took it from him.

"Thanks, AJ."

"Anything for you." He smiled.

As he drove her back to the beach house, Blu reached out and took his hand in hers.

AJ glanced over at her with a subtle wink.

CHAPTER 30

The next day Blu and the kids headed straight out to the beach. She hoped that some sunshine would soothe her nerves from the night before. With Jack behind bars, she didn't have to be afraid, but she wanted more than that. She wanted to laugh and to smile. She wanted to find summer again.

"Look at my castle, Blu." Marley danced around a big mound of sand with a shell on top.

"It's beautiful, Marley. You know what it needs, though?"

"What?" Marley scrunched up her nose.

"A moat." Blu smiled. She picked up a bucket. "Let's go get some water."

"Yes!" Marley giggled. She ran straight to the water.

Blu jogged to keep up with her. She dipped the bucket into the water and filled it to the brim. As Blu toted it back to the mound of sand, Marley skipped beside her. Together they dug out a circle around the mound.

"Here, you pour the water in." Blu helped Marley tip the bucket. The water rolled through the circle to surround her castle.

"Hm. Know what it needs?" Marley tapped her chin.

"What?" Blu smiled.

"Fishies!" Marley giggled.

"Oh, good idea." Blu nodded. "Maybe we can find some in the water." She took Marley's hand and began to walk with her, back toward the water. Before they'd reached the edge of the waves, a voice drew Blu's attention.

"Blu?"

She looked up to see Marta and Oliver beside the beach chair she'd just left. "Just a minute, Marley. We have some friends here to visit with." Blu led the little girl back to Marta and Oliver. "Hello." She smiled at them.

Marta's hand looked like it was clasping Oliver's so tightly that Blu wondered if it hurt him.

"I'm sorry if this is intrusive." Marta cleared her throat. "It's just that Oliver and I both wanted to thank you for everything that you did."

"Everything that I did?"

Oliver nodded.

Marta glanced away shyly. "I know we didn't make it easy. We didn't give you an inch. But you still fought for us. If you hadn't done that—well, I'd be getting ready for my trial right now."

"Don't even think that." Oliver frowned. "I can't

imagine what would have happened. Now my mother is in jail, my father is gone…" He blinked and shook his head. "If someone would have told me that this was what was coming, I never would have believed them. Blu, without you, the truth wouldn't have come out."

"I'm just sorry that you had to go through it all in the first place." Blu frowned as she met Marta's eyes. "You tried so hard to live a life that was different than your family's."

"When I found out that Hilda went to Juan for a way to get Emile out of her life, I knew that he was going to get in over his head. He tried to tell me that all he had to do was create a letter—fake a lawsuit. He didn't think it was a big deal. If only I'd gotten there a little earlier, maybe I could have done something to stop all of it." She looked over at Oliver. "I wish I had."

"And if only I had gone up on the top of the lighthouse—or if my father had felt that he could tell me the truth about the letter he'd received—maybe I could have saved him. But the truth is, there's only one place to lay the blame and that's on the man who put his hands on my father. Of course, my mother was the one who planned it, so she shares that blame. I'd like to think that she didn't mean for him to die, but I know better—all of the fighting over the years, all the distance between them. The signs were there. I just didn't want to see them."

"What are you two going to do now?" Blu looked from one to the other. "I hope all of this won't stop you from doing what you truly want."

"It won't." Marta smiled. "We're going to start our lives—brand new—together. Right, Oliver?"

"Right." Oliver looked into her eyes. "The way we feel about one another kept us strong throughout all this, and we're not going to let that slip away."

Blu recalled what Marta had said in the interrogation room about love not always being enough. It was clear that Marta had changed her mind.

"I'm glad. I wish you both the best."

"Thank you, Blu." Marta met her eyes. "You saved my life, and I will never forget that."

Blu smiled as the two walked away. She blinked back a few tears and returned with Marley to her castle.

"Blu, can I please?"

Blu looked up in the direction of Joey's voice. "Can you what?"

She turned to see where Joey was pointing. AJ was walking toward them with two surfboards tucked under his arms.

"Hey, Blu. I thought maybe I could show Joey some moves on the water. Nothing too crazy. What do you think?"

Blu smiled. "I think that would be wonderful."

"Yes!" Joey ran toward the water with AJ right behind him.

Blu watched the two walk toward the water with the smile still on her face. Maybe if Marta was willing to change her mind about love and take a risk, Blu could take that risk too.

Maybe.

ALL TITLES BY MACI GRANT

http://Amazon.com/author/macigrant
*Check the author page for current list of titles

Summer in Diamond Bay

#1 Lifeguards and Liars
#2 Sandcastles and Secrets
#3 Ice Cream and Intrigue
#4 Hot Dogs and Homicide
#5 Clambakes and Chaos